0·10

A Funny Old Year

First published in the United Kingdom by

Dewi Lewis Publishing

8 Broomfield Road, Heaton Moor

Stockport SK4 4ND, England

+44 (0)161 442 9450

www.dewilewispublishing.com

ISBN: 1-899235-63-9

Printed and bound in Great Britain by
Biddles Ltd, Guildford and King's Lynn

2 4 6 8 9 7 5 3 1

A Funny Old Year

Alan Brownjohn

DEWI LEWIS
PUBLISHING

for Roger Jerome

Come sir, it wants a twelvemonth and a day,
And then 'twill end.
Love's Labour's Lost

Sleep well – and wake up to sunshine –
There's sunshine – tomorrow – for you!
Old Song

'Tell me. What do you see?'

'I can see nothing.'

'Nothing? You are absolutely certain you see *nothing*?'

'Only darkness.'

'Well,' he said eventually, 'I would be astonished if you could see anything. I happen to have covered both your eyes with opaque lenses. My apologies!'

He went about removing one lens from the heavy frame resting on the bridge of my nose.

'You see now over there a red line, yes?'

'I do, Dr Koning.'

'More to the right? Or to the left?'

'The left.'

'Excellent, Mr Barron! Your speciality is politics, and you still can tell the left from the right. That is becoming harder these days.'

I managed an affirming smile, though it was an effort. After the many years I had been coming to see Koning I thought of him as almost a friend. And yet he retained a German formality which threw his small sallies of quirky humour into a sharper relief.

'Now read those letters for me, Mr Barron,' he instructed, pointing at the wall opposite, where the chart of diminishing capitals shone out with its challenges. 'Loud and clear.'

'M...Y, R...O, F, T...' I completed the exercise except for the final row of tiny letters at the foot, which I could not begin to decipher.

'Very good. But you memorised them last time, yes?'

'I did *not*.'

'Won't you *try* the bottom line?'

'R... O... Is it S? I can't tell what the end –'

'If you could, you would be exceptional, Mr Barron. It's remarkable for people to know all of their bottom line. They delude themselves if they think they know even their penultimate line.'

But I had managed my own penultimate line. And I said so, protesting with a laugh.

'Yes, I know. I know. You have done splendidly. You are able to see the wood, if not the trees. I need perhaps to help you with the trees.' Now he too smiled, in a comparatively relaxed and amiable fashion, as if in contented anticipation of his next trick. 'So we shall try the seasons, with the help of your Mr Shakespeare.' He put into my hand a card with prose and verse passages in different type-sizes. 'Read No.4 to me, loud and clear. Or sing it if you prefer.'

I did not wish to sing for Dr Koning. I merely set out to read it, rather slowly and quietly:

> 'When daisies pied, and violets blue,
> And cuckoo-buds of yellow hue:
> And lady-smocks all silver-white
> Do paint the meadows with delight,
> The cuckoo then –'

'Louder! More confidence! I want to *see* those flowers. I want to *hear* that bird, Mr Barron.'

Playing his game, I almost shouted the cuckoo calls that followed. Again he smiled, this time quite warmly and generously.

Unless he was being sardonic.

'But this is magnificent,' he assured me. 'The performance, I mean.'

Having got used to his humour (it had taken numerous consultations), I liked this man, I believed in him. But he could still be disconcerting.

'So how is your wife?' he turned and asked me suddenly.

He had a good memory. He was referring to Rosie, who had accompanied me here last time.

'That was not my wife. I am not married,'

'Ah...' He paused, reflectively. 'I am sorry. I have thought you *might* be married.' He shook his head, not in disapproval of my bachelor status but, I felt sure, in genuine self-reproof for forgetting about it. 'Well, then. Enough! Our explorations reveal that from now on you may forget your distance spectacles!'

I smiled with a surprise and a pleasure he appeared to appreciate.

'Forget them altogether? Even for driving?'

'Even for that. But we want to see the trees as well as the wood, do we not? Old age has made you a far-sighted fellow, but you need a clearer picture of the things under your nose. How old *are* we, Mr Barron?'

'Fifty-eight.'

'Middle age, then. Nearly the same as myself. So... Let's see what we can offer you...'

❊

That was at the end of July last year. What follows is the story of the twelve curious months between that visit to 'Dr C. Koning: Ophthalmic Surgeon' and the present. And in some ways I am surprised to be still alive and writing it down for you to read.

You already know my name is Barron. In full, it's Michael Charles Barron. I am, as Dr Koning established, fifty-eight years old, and still an active man. And if you think that implies an interest in women, you would be right.

I shall be giving the story of my arrangement with Rosie, which will have come to a conclusion by the last pages of this account. And covering a number of other matters. I shall tell you about my friend Geoff Stedman, which will bring in Dr Hulzer the Director, Reginald Torridge his dancing Deputy, Dave Underhill, Head of HELSACS, and Dennis Frostick; all of these being figures at the Polytechnic where Geoff and I taught for so many years, and from which we were successively fired. There are also younger persons, like Jane and Bill Bramston and their teenage children Zilla and Rory. Jane, a former student of mine at the Polytechnic, now a University, no less, and (yes) a very good friend, was a special reason for my choosing to live where I do, in this small English holiday town, during my 'year of trial'.

The Bramstons have an acquaintance I don't much like, called Trevor Ridyard. And, friend to no one, there is Greg, barman at the Old Soldier, and stalker. Which brings me to Flamingo, who works in the post office and has an important role in this narrative; and she reminds me of the Vic Tillinghurst Quartet. Zilla Bramston reminds me of Treazy and Treazy reminds me of my dentist, Fred Faulkner. I do not have a lot of hair left, but I am not bald, whether by design or accident, and so I visit Ken Trench, the barber in town, and hear his commentaries on local life.

Most all, though, there is Rachel. And more of Rachel quite soon.

So. A fortnight after that visit to Dr Koning I had collected my new reading glasses and was driving back from his consulting rooms in the city where I used to teach in what Stedman called 'our God-stricken Polytechnic' towards the coast and my new residence. This was an over-large Edwardian end-of-terrace property which I was temporarily renting, and had a goodish chance of purchasing if I finally chose to.

The arrangement between Rosie and myself needs a little elaboration and elucidation. She had been widowed in the June just over a year before this, and her loss had shocked us both into

10

wondering if (or how, or when) we could decently continue the relationship – well, call it the affair – we had been having on and off for two or three years before that sad event.

We had had deep discussions during the months thereafter, when it was becoming only too clear to me that my days on the staff of the Polytechnic were numbered. Rosie rapidly became very insistent that if we did resume our connection we should be 'serious' about it, and consider making it permanent. I said that we needed time to decide that, but found myself yielding in the end (because part of me thought that Rosie might be right) to the idea of a 'year of trial'.

We would live some distance apart to see whether we wanted or needed each other enough to make a life together, possibly in marriage. The test would be a genuine one, perhaps involving a firm resistance of other temptations. The terms of our agreement included never meeting, never telephoning, only writing short necessary letters about our movements in case we needed to be in touch for any urgent reason. At the first anniversary of our agreed separation each would write to the other with a decision. If either had decided against a life together, the rejection would not be questioned and we would then go off for ever in different directions.

Returning from the city that day, I felt fit and clear-headed, happy at the prospect of the months ahead. Autumn by the sea would be pleasant, and once over the perilous hump of Christmas I would be into the cold, sun-cleansed months of January and February, looking forward to spring and moving in the direction of a sensible, considered judgement concerning Rosie and myself.

Without the aid of distance glasses (Koning was right) I could read the sticker in the rear window of the Range Rover in front as I followed it along the City's endless Ring Road. It said: TO EACH HIS OWN SAMARRA. What on earth did that mean?

Soon the outlying industrial estates finished and the undulating countryside arrived. I passed fields where the wheat of the summer had been reaped and big bales of straw stood spaced out like immense cotton reels, looking as if a wind could start them rolling. It was five in the afternoon, and when I reached the coast I could do something my working life in that city never allowed me to do: choose, between going straight to the house, or to the pub, the Old Soldier – or to the beach.

I decided on the beach, didn't I, Rachel! And by taking that minor decision I met you for the first time. But there is something else to mention first, quite a small thing but it matters later on.

About four miles short of the sea on this route, the grass verge widens and allows the intersection with the highway of the local Roman road, known as 'Dibdin Street'. At this point you can park, go and exercise a dog if you must, stroll as far as you like along a rough track towards the coast one way, or into the heart of Middle England in the other direction.

There were no parked cars that afternoon, only a couple of bicycles tethered to the 'Public Footpath' sign by a single plastic chain. I had slowed up behind a tractor, and had time to recognise an unmistakeable machine, Bill Bramston's very old and battered blue bike, which he rarely used and had been trying to sell. Here it was then, sold, and providing pleasure for a new owner. I would tell Bill I had seen it.

But I never did tell him.

No, no need for distance glasses as I crested this hill above the sea and took in the panorama: low-lying saltmarsh over to the right, in front the long esplanade, and this side of the esplanade, the town. Everything was finely- and brightly-detailed to my naked eye: the Horizon Theatre, where I would sometimes spend solitary half-hours over cups of tea in the afternoons, the Clifftop Continental Hotel where Jane was Catering Manager, the Lighthouse Museum on the Green, the Old Soldier at the top of the High Street – I could even make out the roofs of Bill's and Jane's street, parallel to that. The sight of the pub reminded me of why I was rejecting it as first choice on this sunny afternoon: I had no drinking companion in this place. My last steady one had been Geoff Stedman, and I shall explain Geoff first before I come to Rachel.

Geoff once said that even his friends and allies misunderstood him. That might have been true of me, but all I know is that he and I happily shared political opinions, and Geoff's friendship was for many years my life-support system at the Polytechnic, a corrective to the pomposity and insanity of the place.

He taught English Literature, and I was 'Lecturer in Politics, with Auxiliary Modules' in the Faculty of Human, Educational, Linguistic, Social and Contemporary Studies, or HELSACS. That title, though not the acronym, had been suggested by Stedman in a memo to a particular enemy, Reginald Torridge, when the Polytechnic required a name to satisfy all the warring interests in the unwieldy new department. Torridge had taken it seriously and passed it through the Academic Board.

Torridge. He had been a lifelong pillar of the Polytechnic as a student, a graduate researcher in organic chemistry, then Lecturer and Senior Lecturer, finally Deputy Director. All that time he had also run the BDS, the Ballroom Dancing Society, teaching it in fashion and out of fashion (and there were still many takers even in the heyday of disco), with the aid, chronologically, of 78s, LPs, EPs, tapes, CDs, instruction videos.

Stedman loathed the BDS. It was a principle with him. He said it 'stood for the closing down of minds, *death* as against *life* in the works of Shakespeare, Wordsworth, George Eliot and Lawrence'. Was this loathing apparent to Torridge? Did it help, along with Geoff's principled defence of everything he believed worth teaching (against the upper and lower jaws of Torridge's conservatism and Dave Underhill's 'progress'), did it help produce the conspiracy between Torridge and Underhill, boss of HELSACS, to abolish Geoff's post? Probably.

Seeing the Old Soldier, I thought of the Drayhorse, across the Games Field adjoining the Polytechnic. I thought of Geoff, set in his adversarial stance, coming out from behind the table in his room, lighting his new cigarette from the last one with angry, trembling hands, humorously cursing the barbarism of the age and suggesting we go to the Drayhorse for a lunchtime drink. Perhaps to end up having one of what we called our 'fucking' conversations. Which I shall explain later.

I am not really the right man to praise and commemorate

Stedman. Not a suitable man, for good reasons. But no one else will; and as he was my friend (I don't think *I* was adequately *his* friend) I shall do what I can.

But now for Rachel.

✳

Unknowingly I was walking along the sand towards her, and the sea brought to mind my father. This is – we are – a maritime nation. That was a maxim of my father's. After the age of thirteen I hardly ever took in his maxims. But one day I started to listen, amazed, when he added a further observation on the same theme.

'There are a lot of sailors can't swim.' he said. 'The ship is the point, not the water.'

Perhaps my father was consoling me for my inability to swim. I still can't, well not properly. But if he was doing that, it would have run contrary to another repeated maxim spoken to encourage me: All you might need in an emergency is the ability to swim the width of a public baths.

On the beach I just walk, then; considerable distances. And jog. But not swim. Not by choice, anyway. Dear Flamingo... But it's too soon to get into all that.

When I walk on this expansively wide and flat beach at low tide I often look to see if a long, unbroken, perfect wave arrives. Many waves are partial successes, but don't complete an unbroken approach; they abandon themselves on the brink of success. Just after starting out that afternoon I witnessed one of the best waves I had ever seen, I swear it was a hundred yards long and uniformly a foot high along its crest, a perfect light grey-green ruff coming in as if it had deliberately slowed itself for a camera to catch. It spread out in front of me for those two seconds like an ideal hand of cards. Rachel's wave.

On this beach, too, you see chunks of sea-smashed wall, relics of wartime lookout posts. I sat down on one, took my new glasses out of

14

my shirt pocket (bad habit to keep them there), relished the exactness of their fit, and read Rosie's first brief practical letter:

Dear Mike,
Just to let you know I shall be going down to
Mother's for the rest of August. Hoping all is fine,
Rosie.

This impeccably observed every rule of our agreement. When I put it back in my wallet I looked up at the horizon through Dr Koning's aids to close-up vision, and saw a satisfying blur. I took the glasses off, and re-focused my gaze with my improved far-sightedness. And saw a solitary, intriguing female dot on the huge stretch of utterly yellow sand. She-who-was-to-be-Rachel was sitting about two hundred yards away to my right.

Female, immediately? No. When I first saw the figure it could have been a piece of sea-wrack, or a lump of brick and concrete of the kind on which I rested. But then it moved. And it was human, and uncontrovertibly female in the way it repositioned its legs. In its loneliness I was drawn to it. I was lonely myself.

I ambled in that direction as if I was any idle summer stroller. Yes, this was a bent, intent female figure which once or twice stretched its arms out in front of her (I could see it well enough to say 'her' now) as she sat cross-legged in her shorts on the sand. Tall; I guessed that from the prominent jut of the tanned knees as she sat there with head down over something she was writing.

Raising my head, I crossed between this tall blonde of about twenty and the ebbing water, in a space ten yards wide. I was an intrusion on her field of vision, but this was better than if I had walked, less reassuringly, behind her. She now looked up. Not at me, I was sure, an unremarkable fifty-eight year old, but at the sea. Or so I thought until much later. I took in the crotch of her shorts, and her sweater. You may not like me for saying this, but I wanted her.

So this encounter, even though Rachel had gone when I absent-mindedly turned round to look back fifty yards farther on, made it

easier for me to feel less lonely without Rosie and reply to her letter
in similarly cool and formal terms.

*

Stedman once said, proposing a principle on which you might
say he finally acted, 'If you must go mad, at least do it in a way that
entertains your friends.' But a few weeks after my first sighting of
the unforgotten blonde on the beach, I began to think that my rented
accommodation might drive me not entertainingly but tediously,
insufferably mad in well under twelve months.

It is large. It has three storeys, and is the last in an eight-house
terrace built in gingery sandstone on a side road on the inland
outskirts of the town. There is no sea view, something difficult to
achieve in a place most of which slopes down towards the water, but
nevertheless my house manages it. To the end wall a flight of
wrought-iron steps has been added, leading to a door knocked
through at second-floor level. This door opens onto a primitive
kitchen because someone once contrived to convert all of this floor
into a very basic holiday apartment, grimly decorated with orange
wallpaper and furnished very crudely. You can also enter this flat
from the inside, via a door at the top of a flight of stairs going up
from the landing outside my first-floor bedroom.

Through the front entrance door of the house you enter a musty
hall (coatstand with snapped-off wooden hooks) which ends in a
kitchen with badly-fitting wall cupboards. There is a lounge with
deep, tatty armchairs and pouffes, a dining room with sideboard and
polished table, very inconvenient except possibly for the dinner
parties I would not be giving. No television, but that did not upset me.

I could go on, about the 'sun lounge' that stank of untraceable
damp, the bedroom with bumpy double bed and crumbling gas fire,
the bog operated by pulling on a green sorbo ball at the end of a
chain. I shall not. But one warm Saturday night in September I
came back from a tense drink or two in the Old Soldier and thought

I would have to get out of this building. I stood in a sort of trembling revulsion in the hall for several minutes, then phoned Jane Bramston – who invited me to lunch next day.

When I arrived at Bill and Jane's she was carrying dishes out into their little back garden with its rockery and raised lawn and toolshed, wearing smart, tight-fitting jeans and looking good. Jane was now a bright-mannered thirty-eight with her glowing reddish-brown hair glossy and well-coiffured (and a little dyed?), in keeping, I supposed, with her management responsibilities at the Clifftop Continental Hotel. The pleasures of long acquaintance drew me to her. I was really glad I had come, to eat outside on such a fine day.

Short and full-figured, Jane was such a contrast to her husband. Bill was slightly older, deeply reliable-looking, thin, colourless, a friend from Polytechnic days, unexpected partner for such a lively girl. He had a job in City Hall, to which he commuted on the seventy minutes' drive from here. He had to dress rather officially for his working week so his Sunday clothes were informal and dirty.

But here was something strange... Today, when I greeted her, Jane gave me a long, significant, smile-and-frown look of the old sort, suggesting that she had a personal life situation to tell me about. I hadn't seen such an expression on her face for a long time. Bill was going back into the house to summon the teenagers for lunch, so Jane had a chance to drop her voice and say, 'Mike – when we're *alone* – there are things I'd like to tell you about.' And the realisation that she was still regarding me as a willing listener to her problems broke on my mind with the freshness of Rachel's long wave on the August sands.

But Bill was returning. 'The kids are coming,' he said. And, 'Did you see my new car in the street? Well, not a *new* one, but new for me. Come and have a look before we sit down.'

This was the moment at which I nearly told him I had seen his old blue bike, and fatefully I omitted to do that. I merely admired his new vehicle, which allowed me to recognise it in other places later: a spacious light grey Volvo estate. I took no special interest.

But yes, I did remember it. A memorable registration number stuck in my mind: 2-3-4.

Jane worked in Catering Management, not catering, and her food was, as usual, unappetising stuff: fridge-cold chicken legs, hard home-made bread, no butter, no salt, no flavour in the shell-shaped pasta still crisp from under-cooking, no life in her salad with its raw cabbage, bits of tinned pineapple, unpeeled apple lumps, segments of tangerine. For dessert she served the same pasta as a thin, milky pudding with a fruit salad of everything in the main course apart from the cabbage. I wondered how fifteen year-old Zilla and twelve year-old Rory looked so healthy, because they ate almost nothing.

'I told you Geoff Stedman died?' I asked; and realised that this was not the case, so I had to recount the details. They both expressed brief shock, and fell silent. News of the death of someone important to your informant but not well-known to you, can be a genuine conversation-stopper. There was a macabre pause in the talk at the table; which Jane finally broke, rather uneasily I thought, by changing the subject.

'We'd like to have you round to meet our friend Trevor Ridyard, wouldn't we, Bill. You'd like him.'

So why should I like this Trevor Ridyard? I might be lonely here, but that was intentional; I was supposed to be thinking profoundly about Rosie and myself. There was a limit to the sociability I wanted to produce for strangers. I did not want to be sucked into a round of invitations, obligations. Instinctively I felt cautious about this new name.

✳

After the meal we went on sitting among the dishes at the table in the garden, but the sun was shining as if summer had decided not to end at all, even though it was the penultimate Sunday of September. And so, at about three-thirty I gave my thanks and apologies to Jane and Bill and told them I would go and get some desirable exercise on the beach.

As we walked back through their house to the front door and the street, the phone rang and Bill doubled back to answer it. As soon as he was out of sight Jane took my hand.

'What it is,' she said quietly, with no introduction, as if seventeen years had not passed since her last startling confidences, 'is Bill's been taking peculiar photographs.'

I took a few seconds to register this sudden, whispered revelation.

'What do you mean by "peculiar"?' I remembered Jane's propensity for exaggeration and fantasy.

'What else would I mean?' As if I was a child.

'You mean – women?'

'I've been finding them.'

'Are they women you know?'

'Christ, of course not!' She laughed scornfully. 'Mike, call again soon, won't you?'

'Of course I will. Why don't you call on me?' But I thought of the house and half hoped she would not.

'There's so little time... And it's not very easy anyway.'

'Try. Please. You've things to tell me, I think? Haven't you!'

'Yes, I probably have.'

Reaching the beach I strolled along until I could see no one between myself and the land horizon. This time the tide was in, the high sand soft and difficult to walk on. I scrambled up a dune to a place where there was a long walkway of wooden planks laid down between the saltmarshes and the sea, some fifteen feet above the shore. Probably this path was for birdwatchers, but I was just a stroller, not legitimised by binoculars and a tripod, let alone a dog.

I clattered along for about five minutes, suddenly feeling old and suspicious-looking. Then I stopped to read a notice:

This area of dune is older and more stable than that nearer the sea. Because of the large number of mosses and lichens, it has a greyish appearance and hence is known as a grey dune. Deposits of millions of seashells also contribute to that effect.

19

Or vast deposits of half-cooked pasta?

I stopped and sat down on the slope of a dune where I could relax, in a private corner screened by reeds and marram grass. Far out on the sea were two yachts, white triangles balanced on the tightrope of that horizon, an invisible line between the dark blue mass of the water and the untouched lighter blue of the afternoon sky. The sun blazed, nothing autumnal about it, on me and on them. Surely when the autumn did come it would be a handsome season.

When I fractured the surface of the firm sand at my side the grains ran down in a small avalanche to be halted by friction. My hand cast a shadow over the late summer insects crawling and stumbling over the shifted sandgrains; I took my newish glasses out of my shirt pocket to have a closer look at them.

Out above the sea the pilot of a tiny plane, a craft smaller than anything mechanical I had ever seen flying, might have had the same feeling as I had, poised on a vantage point over life past and life to come. But I didn't have to fly to feel it. I was an old and stable man contented on an old and stable dune. And alone here.

Except for one single female cough. Someone lightly coughing and clearing her throat just round the corner. I knew this person was also alone. Had there been other people, even one, there would have been other sounds before this. Besides, the breaking of half-an-hour's silence would have come with someone else's reaction. An echoing cough, a remark.

There was no dog with this person, I would have seen it. That is not as irrelevant as it might seem. Most people coming here by themselves were bringing the dog. Dogs caused them to be here. Dogs validated them. Dogs ruled out any thought that they might be undesirables. Dog-walking is healthy and moral, peculiar people don't do it. A dogless man of unblemished virtue and innocent intention could be branded a homicidal sex-maniac by a dog-lover in paranoid mode. Someone whistling up a dog here could be the worst kind of pervert imaginable and go unsuspected.

The cough I heard was a preparation for moving. There was a purposeful intake of breath as someone stood up. And when she emerged and passed across a yard or two in front of me, carrying a notebook, she showed no surprise. It was almost as if she had expected to see me.

Legs, shorts, hips, sweater, hair: Rachel, as she was soon to be, was imposingly beautiful and about the same age as most of my freshwomen at the Polytechnic, girls I would have been meeting this time of year had I still been there. I looked at her in a practised and calculating neutral-but-not-unfriendly way.

And she returned my look.

And she uttered words, and smiled slightly.

'See you later,' was what she said.

✳

Late September. Freshwomen.

The week that to me meant an unwelcome return to work relieved (hugely or only a little, according to the crop) by the arrival of a set of first-year girls, ever younger and more distant and therefore all the more sexually attractive, was for Geoff Stedman the eager beginning of another teaching mission: the genuine educationalist's New Year.

'I'm not in this just for the cash, essential as that is,' he said once. 'Or for an intellectual pastime, unlike Dave Underhill.' But did I really grasp what Stedman was talking about? What his 'values' and 'standards' and 'canon' meant? What promoting 'life' was, and exactly how it made him look for enemies, leave HELSACS faculty meetings vibrating with fury after learning of some dictatorial decision handed down by Reginald Torridge – 'another load of ballroom dancing!'?

Geoff could not have been picked out in any crowd as a remarkable individual. In the days when I took out my Politics students on 'vox populi' interview projects during, say, the 1982 Falklands War or the 1984-5 Miners' Strike, I would never have stopped Geoff in the hope of a fruitful exchange. He just wouldn't have seemed interesting enough to bother with.

No more than about five-foot four, he was thickly built, with black untidy hair and a moustache which compounded the ordinariness of a small, rather crushed red face with bulging cheeks. His solid-rimmed spectacles he took off for reading, which he did with the book held close to his face, increasing the impression he gave of almost manic intentness on any given text. In class, students said, he would read aloud like that, the words gushing out over the top of the book with volcanic heat. But intermittently he would lower the volume to his lap and carry on from memory, in a loud, precise baritone projected from the depths of his 'teaching armchair'. When particularly stirred, he would leap up and pace the floor, reading and shouting out amiable but challenging questions.

'That guy Stedman's mad, but he's onto something,' a student said as she sat down next to me one lunch time in the refectory. I asked her what she meant, and she said it would need a bit of explaining with the book open. She laid her copy of the poems of John Keats on the table and found the 'Ode on Melancholy', a poem I had never read, and pointed to lines where the poet speaks of the loveliness of a mistress with 'peerless eyes' (I am a Politics lecturer, but that kind of poetry I can definitely understand). She told me Keats was referring to 'Melancholy' itself when he wrote 'She'.

> *She dwells with Beauty – Beauty that must die;*
>   *And Joy, whose hand is ever at his lips*
> *Bidding adieu; and aching Pleasure nigh,*
>   *Turning to Poison while the bee-mouth sips:*
> *Ay, in the very temple of Delight*
>   *Veil'd Melancholy has her sovran shrine,*
>   *Though seen of none save him whose strenuous tongue*
> *Can burst Joy's grape against his palate fine...*

At that point, the student said, two lines from the end of the great Ode, Stedman stops his quiet, deep delivery of the lines and says,

'O.K., O.K., who's ever tried to burst a grape against his or her 'fine' palate with just his or her tongue? Strenuous or otherwise?'

From the drawer of his desk he produces a small bag of fresh black grapes, and they all try to do it, and no, they can't. Grapes are solider than you think. So then Stedman says, 'It might be possible to do it with an over-ripe, nearly rotten grape. But Keats wasn't thinking of those. He's thinking of a grape as fresh as these. So we have a choice, yes? Either we say he's been careless with his metaphor and not thought through his idea properly. Or we don't take the notion of the grape too literally but accept it (it produces wine, and so on) as a symbol of Joy that only a *very* special person can appreciate, the one in a hundred thousand with a tongue – all the associations with the power of words, language, etc – a tongue strong enough to break through to that Joy and know it fully, consequently know the Melancholy waiting inside the fruit. That very special being is Keats himself, is, if you like, the Romantic artist. Comments, please!'

Next they went on to Keats's 'To Autumn', but I forget what was told about Stedman's interpretation of that, except that it was passionate and extraordinary.

＊

Time was already moving quite quickly. Did I say I had been hoping for a 'pleasant', a 'handsome', autumn here by the sea?

After the lustrous September came an October of lashing, lacerating rain. A damp stain on the wall in the sun lounge began to spread, but I could not be bothered to show it to my landlord, thinking that the house was not going to be somewhere I could bear for very long, even in the event of Rosie joining me here and moving into it. The rent was reducing my savings, but using them to purchase it seemed inconceivable. 'Will you be renting out the flat upstairs?' the landlord had asked when I gave him the first quarter's amount in advance; probably hoping that a tenant would keep it conveniently heated. But how on earth would I find anyone to take it on in the winter months?

One Thursday lunchtime I went down to the High Street in the rain and had my hair cut. I asked Ken Trench, the barber, about the prospects of finding someone to whom I might sublet a spacious top-floor apartment.

He gave me a merry, cynical smile in the mirror.

'You might advertise it in the Gazette and News,' he said. 'But you'd have regrown this lot –' patting my mainly bald head – 'before anyone phoned you.' I thought this was insensitive. 'Although,' he went on, 'if you put it with a short breaks agent and only asked a peanut for it, you'd stand a slightly better chance of someone taking it for a dirty week-end. And you'd help local business, because there's not much other trade at this time of year.'

Ken was refusing to take my question seriously, so I tried to get back at him.

'You aren't doing too well yourself?' I suggested. I was the only person in his salon on this wet late morning.

'See that?' He pointed to a photograph on his wall of a young male, a garishly white face covered, except for its open, singing mouth, with long braided strands of chestnut hair. 'He's a regular.'

Obviously I was expected to know who he was, and to accept that he might represent business and prestige enough as his hairdresser to keep Ken Trench alive. I dug into the depths of my memory of news in the local paper for some rejoinder to this information, Ken's reference to my thinness on top having hurt me more than I expected.

'He's not one of the local Satanists?'

Ken stopped and looked at me over my head in the mirror with scissors open.

'Not funny,' he said. And yet he smiled. 'It's Vin Temple, of the Minjies.'

'Are they popular round here?' I asked, still unsure what Ken was referring to.

'Stronger round here than the Tories these days,' he replied.

Outside again I made for the Old Soldier, despite some trepidations about its barman, and was almost at once stopped in the rain by a short, hooded, hurrying figure.

'Mike! Where have *you* been for three weeks?'

Brooding, fantasising in a dreadful rented house about lonely girls on beaches. And yes, it had been three weeks. I couldn't tell Jane 'at home' because it didn't feel like 'home'.

'Have you time for a drink and a bite? Please! I'd like that talk we were going to have.'

I thought she spoke over-eagerly somehow, but I was pleased with the idea and agreed without hesitating.

'In your bar?' The bar of the Clifftop Continental, where she worked. She shook her head firmly; this, we had said, was probably not a place where we should be seen together too often. 'The Old Soldier?'

It was my 'local', I suppose, but any original affection I had for the place had drained away. It was a quiet, well-stocked, old-fashioned pub, but out of season the staring local clientele made it uncomfortable for a stranger like myself. And above all, there was Greg.

Today Greg stood in his usual position at the bar, black-bearded and glaring, hugged by a heavy navy-blue sweater, ominous and unhelpful in manner, taking my drinks order, which I gave with a smile, with only the curtest nod of silent acknowledgement, agreeing with bad grace to 'see about' a sandwich. It was as if he grudged the pub being open at all.

I believed I could trace his resentment of me to a couple of extremely minor incidents on the same day back in August. First I troubled him to change a twenty pound note in paying for a half-pint of lager. Then, about fifteen minutes later, he was behind me in the queue at the post office. That was inside Consumerama, the large department store in the middle of the High Street, at the back of the ground floor. The younger of the two assistants who served there was a girl of quite exceptional, silently elegant loveliness; startlingly tall (taller than me, and I am five-foot eleven), and with a delicate grace

of movement that was curiously bird-like. I began to think of her as
'Flamingo'.

I had tried once or twice to engage Flamingo in light
conversation, without any success, and on the day in question I
suppose I could have been taken to be 'chatting her up.' All I know
is that when I had finished, and moved aside to put a stamp on a
postcard, Greg pushed forward and elbowed space for himself with
an abrupt 'Do you mind!' and began an intense conversation of his
own with her. After that he had a scowling, threatening look
whenever he saw me at his bar.

'I've come across more,' Jane whispered when I brought the drinks.

'More what?'

'*Photos*!' As if the answer was obvious, and I should have
remembered at once. 'He keeps them in different drawers. Some
were stashed away inside sweaters. And last week I thought there
was something bumpy about the spare room carpet. When I lifted it
he'd hidden about twenty new ones underneath.'

I shook my head in compassionate amazement.

'You haven't told me what they are. They're not – pornographic?'

'No. Just snaps – of these women. On the beach. Or no – mostly
in streets. I think those are near where he works, City Hall area. It
may be when he goes out to lunch. Quite nice, some of them.'

'But what are they doing?'

'That's it! Just walking...'

'So nothing really peculiar?'

'No. Well, except that they all have their backs to the camera. He
has to be afraid they'll see him taking them. I think he spots them
coming towards him, turns his back as if he's fiddling with the
exposure or something, and when they've just passed...' She made a
little frame, a couple of feet from my face, with the forefingers and
thumbs of her two hands, and clicked her teeth.

'But – why?'

'Some are very fetching. Short skirts and tidy little bums.'

'I wouldn't have imagined Bill had that side to him. Have you got
any with you?'

26

'No, I...'

'Your sandwiches!' Greg, not prepared to walk the few paces required to bring them to us, even though we were the only customers, slapped the plate on the bar. Now Jane looked at her watch. But hadn't we just arrived?

I went to collect the sandwiches, and as I turned round with them from the bar I saw Jane staring across my line of gaze to the swing doors through which we had entered, as if in anticipation. And then I saw those two door-halves aggressively pushed apart and a man come in. A very odd figure indeed.

As if he was dismally short-sighted, this bustling little creature in green baseball cap hiding his eyes, drenched anorak open to show a woolly sweater, and crumpled, stained jeans, directed the peak of his headgear into every corner before spotting Jane. Who was waving to him.

Trevor Ridyard, as he turned out to be, plodded across to her in his trainers with ungainly little steps and seemed about to greet her with warm relief. But she rose and came very deliberately over to me for salt and pepper from the bar. It made it clear to Trevor that someone else was with her.

'Surprised to see you here,' he mumbled implausibly to Jane. I received a hostile look from him; and how did I know, before he hauled off his ample cap, that Trevor Ridyard would be bald? Baldness was, I suppose, on my mind after my visit to the barber; but that would not explain it.

I have nothing against bald men. For some time I have almost been one, though the hair loss has apparently halted, leaving me with enough thin strands across the crown of my head to claim that I am *not* bald. What I think I am saying is that there are those whose baldness you can't sense when they wear something on their heads, and those whose baldness you *can*.

Did Trevor's baldness just follow logically from the rest, was that how I knew? Not only from the clothes but also from the rimless glasses and the moustache no wider than the exceptionally narrow nostrils, and the fixed nasty expression? At any rate, when he took

27

off the cap and shook rain onto the carpet Trevor was wholly, deliberately, gratuitously, shamelessly bald, though with a coating of stubble. And not my kind of chap in the least.

Jane gave a little formal introduction, and for a moment I thought, Has this drink and sandwich been contrived especially to get me to meet Trevor Ridyard? Did I radiate a loneliness abject enough to warrant *that*?

'Ooh, I've heard a fair bit about *you*!' Trevor exclaimed, nasally and without warmth. He didn't seem to notice my hand held out in greeting.

'Favourable things, I hope?'

'Ooh yeah! All the Polytechnic stuff.' He grinned, not at all nicely, looking me in the eye. He sat down now, with a bump, and took one of the sandwiches without asking.

'So what do you do yourself?' I could challenge him that much as he had been implicitly unpleasant about my late occupation. Was he twenty-five? Fifty-five? A deck-chair attendant? A warehouse-man at Consumerama?

He laughed, and smoothed his head with a thick hand.

'Ooh – a good question. What *do* I do?' He grinned now at Jane. Perhaps I had embarrassed a man down on his luck. I felt slightly mean. All the same, sympathy didn't allow me to offer Trevor Ridyard a drink. Then suddenly I knew that he was not just embarrassed by my question but uncomfortable about my being there at all.

Jane must have sensed that I was proposing to drink up and leave, because she placed a hand on mine as I reached out for my glass. 'Don't go yet,' she said. I felt a little better, reassured to be wanted.

Thus, before I could stop myself, I said to Trevor,

'What will you drink?'

'Thank you. A double brandy if it's all right with you – Mike.'

Greg, who had nothing else to do, had been watching us all this time, though I think he was too far away to have heard our conversation. But seeing me approach, he turned his back and busied himself by shuffling bottles and glasses on a ledge. I put a five pound note down, audibly, on the bar and he swung round slowly to face me with brooding, contemptuous eyes. His dilatoriness in executing the delivery of the double brandy gave me time to turn in a casual way, and glance over at the corner table where the three of us were sitting.

When I did I saw Trevor lean or slump forward. He pulled a wallet out of his back pocket. Out of it he took something, not money, not paper of any kind, something else which I could not see, and dropped it in Jane's hand.

*

When I finally left them in the Old Soldier the sun was shining, with a hint that it might go on doing that for the rest of the afternoon.

I believe I can think while I walk. Today I wanted to think, because in my pocket was a postcard from Rosie, the first communication for almost two months, and I had been quite pleased to receive it. I returned to the house for the car, and drove out to that point on Dibdin Street, the Roman road, where I had seen Bill Bramston's old blue bike on that day in August. I parked near an ageing Metro and set out determindedly.

I was soon cursing the mud underfoot, Dibdin Street being charmless and filthy in places because of the rain; but I resolved to go on. I was heading in a northerly direction, towards the sea that is, re-reading Rosie's words, which went up to the boundaries of our agreement.

She had come back from her mother's to feel bored and purposeless, and wished she was still young enough to have her previous job, the administration block being a dull place after so many years of activity. The weather in the city had been damp and disappointing (the place was not so far away that I would be unaware of that) and she envied my freedom from urban pressures. 'Warm regards to you, Mike,' she ended, which I thought was ominous. I decided to reply more staidly than that, although it had

29

been satisfying to know that she was well, and that she had no special excitements (rivals?) to tell me about.

The mud on the track gave way to thick, damp grass. Some water entered one of my shoes. I went back exactly one year to an October day when Geoff Stedman and I were returning from the Drayhorse taking the short cut across the Games Field. Geoff was pitching into Dave Underhill with some vigour, seeing that the supremo of HELSACS had begun putting pressure on his lecturing hours in the cause of (I think it was called) 'organisational realignment'. Either that or 'a more sharply focused structure.' Underhill, who in fact was not much younger than Stedman, was perfectly able to combine a youthful, even revolutionary, image with ruthlessly managerial terminology and attitudes.

As we walked and I listened, we were following another colleague who had left the pub just before us. Dennis Frostick was someone we liked and enjoyed, a weather-tanned lecturer in the geography department who was amiable, unambitious and had an eye for the ludicrous aspects of our workplace, which always helps. He had absolutely no intellectual pretensions, and deferred to the opinions of Humanities staff on their own subjects, not always the custom with Polytechnic colleagues.

Dennis had been about thirty yards ahead of us. But we saw now that he had stopped with unusual abruptness and was looking down at the ground. As we approached him, he turned round and laughed. It was a still, sunny moment after a lot of rain, similar to today, and the loudness of his unexpected laughter still lingers in my memory, as does the sight of him making a gingerly progress back towards us over a certain few yards of grass. When we had come together he was still smiling, joyfully.

'One day,' Frostick said, 'the Polytechnic will be in big trouble with this field.'

He was wearing dark brown, thick-soled brogues, and stamped his considerable left foot on the ground. Water rapidly rose over it. Stedman's shoes and mine were also soaked as we stood there.

'For some freak reason which we'd need a hydrographer to

30

explain,' Frostick said, 'the water-table seems to be curiously high just here. The Polytechnic may have built a multi-million pound five-storey annexe on an unsuitable, not to say risky, site.'

'They thought the land was a bargain at the price,' I recalled.

'Still a tidy margin for the agents,' Dennis grinned. 'And for the consultant and the architect. And the odd councillor, maybe.'

We all three considered the ground in silence, soaked up to our ankles.

'Tim Hulzer and Reginald Torridge won't be to blame,' I said. Stedman smiled, but looked more serious.

'I wonder if they know,' he said.

It was ironical that his happening to tell management about the damp patch on the field helped to cast him even further as someone who spread interfering opinions. It told against him when his post was 'realigned.'

The fields and copses around Dibdin Street steamed. It was uncanny weather for October, the sky a clear blue, midges buzzing round my head, almost a feeling of summer heat returning. I enjoyed walking on this utterly straight, gently rising and falling path, watching the layers of landscape slowly uncover themselves, the prospect ahead altering subtly each fifty yards or so. As always I felt drawn forward by this Roman road, obtaining a sense of achievement by so quickly covering distances 'as the crow flies'. When you turn round, the tree you have just passed has fled up to a distant horizon where sky and hedges meet.

And you often meet no one at all, although today I did see an intent treasure-seeker, a grim-faced fellow of around fifty in an old mackintosh, shuffling along and applying his metal-detector to the ground in the hope of finding a reason to dig illegally for Roman silver or gold. I muttered a greeting he did not acknowledge, looked up at the horizon again, strolled on for another ten minutes – and saw that in about another hundred yards I would come face-to-face with she-who-would-now-be-Rachel.

Did she change her rapid, purposeful stride, arms swinging, to a slow stroll purely because she saw me? The space between us diminished much more gradually than I expected. I had time to take in the smart three-quarter length jacket, the leggings hiding the handsome legs (I could vouch for those), the blonde hair down to the collar. I also realised for the first time that she was nearly as tall as me, though not as tall as Flamingo from the post office, another blonde.

I thought, like any adolescent boy, of everything that might ruin this encounter. One of my feet was soaked inside its shoe. I was hatless, and could have been taken as bald. I tried, as she approached, with a gesture that I make so frequently that it has become almost unconscious when I do it for a waitress, or a bank clerk, or a girl at a supermarket check-out, to lift my head so that she would get a full-face first impression and I would not seem so thin on top. That would not be the first thing she noticed.

Long ago a student said to me in bed, 'You know, you are the most calculating man I've ever been involved with. You should have been a politician, not just a Politics lecturer. You can talk your way into anything and out of it again.' I felt flattered, I remember, but didn't reveal how often my calculations went wrong, how the clever talk could dry on my lips. Now, on Dibdin Street in my late fifties, seeking to give a new girl, long dreamt about, a favourable image of myself, I jerked up my chin and a filling fell out of one of my upper back teeth. Not wanting to pluck it out of my mouth and pocket it in front of the lovely and desired stranger, I manoeuvred it into the space between my lower gums and the soft inside of my left cheek.

As she came up, was less than ten yards away, she looked me directly in the face and brightly exclaimed, 'Hullo again, is it far back to the road?' And stopped. Hoarsely and awkwardly, keeping my head high, smiling to make the hint of familiarity in my answer sound natural and friendly, aware my speech was impaired by the raw-tasting chunk of amalgam lodged in my cheek, I answered,

'About half-an-hour's walk.'

'Shit! Have I come as far as that? I'll be in trouble, I really will. Have I seen you in the Horizon Café?'

'I've seen you on the East Beach.'

'Oh right, yes. But I saw you first. In the Horizon. I served there once, in August. You go there to work?'

I was unutterably amazed, because she must have seen me before I had noticed her. Given her looks and my propensities, it was remarkable. But her odd enquiry, Did I go there to work? only puzzled me for a moment. I would usually have been reading a book in a bar or café if I was alone, and she was usually writing in a notebook on the beach. She had identified my lonely activity with her own.

'I go there to think – and work, yes,' I said, not very truthfully, I suppose. We paused, long enough in the sunshine for me to be nearly saying, 'See you there again?' when she looked at her watch.

'He'll be waiting,' she continued, smiling. 'He's been looking for buried treasures as usual. He never finds any.'

'I might have seen him,' I said. Whoever 'he' was. 'About ten minutes ago.'

'Par-dern?' She seemed abstracted.

'Did he have a metal-detector? He was about a mile back.'

'A *mile*?'

'About.'

'Must go and find him. He *is* my Dad. I'm Rachel.'

'What? Oh, my name is Mike. Mike Barron.'

I felt a compulsion to say more. It besets many who spend long periods alone. I resisted it.

'Hullo Mike...' She paused, but still smiled and looked at me. 'Well, then... See you later.'

I can never hear the phrase without thinking I must be due to see the speaker again the same day.

'In the café?' I was thinking on my feet. She raised eyebrows and went on smiling.

'All right. I only served there a couple of days. Let them serve me.'

'I go there most afternoons.' I didn't, but I would now.

'I can go there in the afternoon. Not till the week after next, though.'

'Any particular day?'

'Thursday's O.K.'

'I'll make sure they serve you properly.'

I could scarcely turn round and walk back with Rachel, all the same. Besides, we had made a date. The Horizon Café, above the Horizon Theatre. *We had made a date.*

By the time I was back at the car humid twilight had dimmed to darkness. The old Metro had gone, and presumably the obsessed treasure-seeking Dad and his daughter Rachel with it. There was another car parked beside mine, with a sticker which would have delighted Stedman: 'SOD THE SPONSOR'. It caught my exhilarated, irresponsible mood.

But driving back through the outskirts of the town and along the clifftop avenue, I thought how weather-battered the sea-facing Edwardian buildings looked, how uninhabitable in their winter abandonment after decades without year-round loving attention. The exhilaration gave way to sadness, and worse. I felt there was more than a touch of self-pity about comparing myself with a seafront Edwardian terrace, but that is what I was doing.

Opposite, on the wide cliff-top green. the tea-rooms were shut, the glass-fronted shelters deserted, the museum in the onshore lighthouse dark. But that was strange. From the highest of the tiny slit-windows in the white lighthouse walls, and then from the glass lamp-compartment at the very top, came some very brief flashes of light. It was as if someone had switched on a torch and then just as quickly switched it off again.

✳

Earlier I referred to what I came to think of as the 'fucking' conversations I had with Geoff Stedman. I need to explain about those, and I shall. They came to mind as I sat in a pub Geoff would not have liked at all, a place in the city where I went for a drink after keeping my emergency appointment with Fred Faulkner, my dentist.

'Ah, falling to pieces are we?' I produced the filling, attached to a bit of broken-off tooth. 'Won't need that. Past history now.'

I preferred Koning's clowning to Faulkner's jocular melancholy, though it's fair to say Faulkner rarely provided any conversation at all. But perhaps the dentist's mood was a better preparation for my Horizon Café meeting with Rachel, because he in no way raised my spirits. To go with light heart to the Horizon and find Rachel didn't turn up would be worse than arriving with no great hopes and finding my pessimism justified.

Outside I had parked behind a car with a sticker appropriately showing tragic and comic masks, for a theatre company no doubt. The legend underneath was VITA NOSTRI BREVIS EST, Our life is short. That, as well as Faulkner's gloom, enhanced a suitably despondent mood of my own. I had become obsessed with the idea that Rachel could not begin to think she could get as much out of me as I libidinously hoped to get out of her.

Truly, I had become terrified that she might think I had nothing to repay her with. Not in the narrow sexual sense, because I really did believe I could provide her with *something* in that province. But in terms of relationship, and in regard to the future. Only money or genius or some enthralling extremity of personality captures and retains youthful beauty for old men, and I had none of those things.

A dentist needs to be a good monologuist. Faulkner was given to a brooding, introspective silence, and this time it lasted until almost the end of my forty minutes' treatment. He had reached the stage of smoothing off the material he had packed into my repaired tooth before he suddenly said,

'City's on a downward slope.'

'How?' I asked him, as soon as I had the use of my mouth back. I was sitting up in surprise at so sudden and sweeping a remark. Had I underestimated Faulkner? A sociological observation, a moral reference? It was the most outright statement he had made in ten years' visits. I had taught 'The Modern City' as a political scientist in the Polytechnic, and convinced my students that every modern metropolis was doomed. Even conceivable successes like Toronto or Stockholm were on the slide.

'Going further down week by week,' Faulkner affirmed. 'Down

the drain. Lost 4-nil to United at home on Saturday. One win and two draws in the first eleven matches.'

Whatever the time of day, and whether or not I was driving, I always had a drink after the dentist's, especially if I needed to take my mind off the return of feeling to an anaesthetised jaw. Seeking my usual resort, the Old Red Lion, I found the name had been changed and the place refurbished.

My father's joke pub names of years ago had almost come true, but with none of his simple, innocent style. You did not see his 'Toad and Typewriter', or 'Hen and Helicopter.' You saw names like the one over what used to be the Old Red Lion: the Firkin Beaver.

Geoff Stedman would have walked out of the Firkin Beaver in seconds flat. Amplified music thudded through its empty lounge bar, meaningless lights winked on rows of fruit machines, risqué aphorisms hung in coy frames on its walls. Geoff could only just tolerate the rackety Drayhorse, where we used to go during his last year at the Polytechnic.

One of the signs of Stedman's fury with the world changing into desperation and near-madness was the increasing violence of his antipathies. Everything that fell below the level of the imperishably great (*Hamlet*, the *Prelude*, the late Beethoven, Piero della Francesca) he increasingly dismissed with brutal anger or ironic mirth. And what he thought of as fashionable trivialities were not even worth discussing, could only be written off in one repeated word: Fucking!

There were probably only two or three 'fucking' dialogues between us, but it seemed like more because they are so vivid in my memory, one in particular. The custom was for one of us suddenly to attach the adjective to somebody or something we would surely both agree to despise. The other would concur in the judgement, with a greater emphasis on the word, then attach it to a suggestion of his own.

Example (hypothetical): I might say, 'Did you see that BBC1 thing last night about fucking Noel Coward'? (Coward being a *bête noire* of Stedman's for his snobbery and patent jingoism). 'Yes! *Fucking* Noel Coward! Following the BBC2 feature on fucking

36

Agatha Christie...' I might then shake my head at the feebleness of the world in acclaiming such mediocrity and say, sadly, *Fucking Agatha Christie!'*

Month by month Stedman's exclusion zone was more and more rigorously extended. He was setting up a defiant personal palisade. Less and less often was anyone compassionately let off with 'suspect', or 'mediocre', or 'fourth rate'. Any reference to someone Geoff did not include in his approved list would be greeted by *'That fucker?'* His views seemed to become more extreme the more he became sure that Underhill wanted him out of the Polytechnic.

'Anything worth reading in that?' I asked, joining him late in the Drayhorse one day and finding him deep inside one of the fall-out sections of the *Guardian*.

Stedman replied, without raising his eyes from the newsprint,'In the "arts" pages of this someone is writing seriously about the "hibernating reputation" of that fucker "Bob Dullan." He pronounced the name 'Dylan' that way (he always said) 'out of respect for the noble language of its origin.' Although I didn't entirely agree with his judgement, I played along with him, sensing a lively few minutes ahead.

'You really mean that? You're serious? Fucking Bob Dylan?'

'I am serious. Fucking. Bob. Dullan.'

I produced my own paper, the *New Statesman*.

'You haven't seen this! There's going to be a whole play about fucking Edith Piaf.'

'Fucking – Edith – Piaf?'

'Fucking Edith Piaf.' I nodded, in a resigned, what-is-the-world-coming-to fashion.

There we had to pause, to see what further contemptible icons occurred to us without the help of the post-modern arts pages. This was not always easy, as we were actually ignorant of names representing whole swathes of popular culture of the kind that columnists could intellectualise about. Current rock, for example, was to us a world of crudity and insensitivity and 'cultural destitution' in which we had neither of us focused any particular personalities, treated solemnly in page after page of simian photography and pretentious journalese. We only knew what we hated when it was impossible to avoid hearing it.

So eventually, to keep Stedman going, 'There was someone yesterday trawling up fucking Elvis Presley, yet again,' I ventured. But this was lame and ancient stuff, and Stedman merely nodded.

He seemed to be thinking hard as he drank, considering something very deeply. Finally he said, 'You know Mike, we're missing an entire hinterland of fucking dreck.' He put down his pint on the table and let the *Guardian* fall to the floor.

'Like fucking what?'

'Like fucking Sondheim.'

'*Fucking* Sondheim.' I went along with it. And racked my brain for others. All I could think of saying was, 'Fucking *Les Miserables*!' and he nodded emphatically. Quickly I tried, through association with hit musicals, another name, hardly believing that we hadn't used it before (there was a rule against repetition in these exchanges.) It was a name famous with the coach parties and the Christmas office outings.

When he heard this name Stedman turned himself into what he said Reginald Torridge once became, when someone got the better of him at the end of a long and tiring course planning session: a steaming, lurching pile of inarticulate rage. He clenched his fists and pressed them against his ribs, sent his face scarlet by tightening his neck and jaw muscles, feigned a paroxysmic inability to project even one syllable through open, quivering lips.

And, in the end, raised the fists to the level of his head and higher, shook them in the air, crashed them down on our table spilling our drinks over both our laps. And roaring, in that baritone voice now raised louder than ever it was in the passions of his seminars...

'Fucking – *fucking* – FUCKING ——— ——— ——— '

The tripartite name must have been audible to every corner of the bar, drowning the muzak.

There came immediately an instant of silence throughout the Drayhorse, Stedman having cut short every drinker's last remark.

But it was a silence of surprise, not shock or disapproval. And it lasted for only that instant. Heads did swivel round to look, but they turned away again at once. In indifference. Only the volume (and Geoff at his most dismissive could be stentorian) had momentarily snatched people's attention. Nothing this speaker was saying had offended anyone. Massacre, corruption, perversion, philistinism there might be. But the world was unshockable and inert. Stedman was in revolt against all blandness of taste and opinion, every small failure of cultural will. Yet even his most furious protests were ignored, assimilated. No one came over to reproach, or warn him; or shake his hand either.

'But I'll tell you something more,' he continued, mopping spilt beer from table and trousers. 'We're forgetting the sacred cows of yesterday.'

What did he mean? Who would be shut out if Geoff extended his stern borderline backwards in time?

'Fucking Rodgers,' he said. I did not catch on, so he just nodded and waited. 'And fucking Hammerstein. And *fucking* Cole Porter.'

'Really?' I said. Involuntarily, because I worried about this judgement, though I thought it might be risky to counter my friend's violently censorious mood.

'And let's face it,' he went on, 'fucking Gershwin.'

'*Gershwin?*' I did protest this time. I could hardly believe what he was saying.

'Yes, fucking Gershwin. No merit as a serious composer, third-rate jazzman, negligible dramatist, talent only as a chameleon and a dabbler. Put him down in the Middle Ages and you'd have fucking bankable plainchant. Bring alms to our abbey and dig Brother George.'

In retrospect I wondered whether it was around this time, in the late October of his last year in the Polytechnic, that Stedman began to flip his lid.

＊

Where was I? Oh yes, on my way to meet Rachel in the Horizon Café, the very thought of her lighting up the desert of these November days, inflaming my being with a probably unjustified but very attractive kind of hope. 'There's only one thing more pathetic than an old womaniser,' the boyfriend of one of my women students once said to me (I had no influence on his exam grades, so he felt at liberty to say it), 'and that's a failed old womaniser.'

It hurt, at the time; and if he could see me now he would have reason to smile. Because, where had my time gone? Why had there been so few chances? To think that there was a period when any one of four women would phone me and say, 'Hi! It's me!' and I would have to guess from the voice which one it was.

Already, high over the wider end of the pedestrian precinct outside the Firkin Beaver was a twinkling reindeer pulling a Santa Claus on a sleigh, picked out in hundreds of tiny white and red lights. This did nothing for my mood. In the car I put my foot down and drove fast towards the one element of genuine fascination in my life, pushing a peppermint into the numb side of my mouth to conceal any smell of the pub whisky.

When I bounded up the few stairs to the café above the little theatre and saw Rachel already sitting there I felt pathetically awed and excited. I ordered coffee for her with authority and good humour, she sipped it looking at me over the cup, I smiled and asked her about where she lived with her parents (she told me) and her brother and sister and cats.

She asked me where I lived myself, and I told her, in my excitement perhaps going on in too much detail; but then she was asking questions about it, in a delightfully interested and animated way. At one point (I was taking in every gesture of her hands, every change of expression on her features, you may be sure) a curiously cunning look came over her face and she fixed my eyes very intently, as if something had struck her and caused her to think rather hard and rapidly. But it passed, and never came back.

'You never saw me when I served here?' Rachel suddenly asked.

'I saw you first on the beach.'

40

'Oh yes, you said, didn't you.'

'You intrigued me', I now risked telling her.

'You were walking by yourself on the beach, and sitting there,' she said unexpectedly. 'You are a reader of books.'

'All true,' I said.

'No one else round here reads books,' she observed. 'I go to the library, but...'

Rachel could really have been one of my freshwomen.

'I haven't seen people reading if they do.'

'No one would want to read my book,' Rachel said.

'You've written a book? *I* might like to read it,' I replied.

'I'm writing one now.'

The walls of the Horizon Café were decorated with framed views which you would have met in station waiting-rooms in the 1950s: sepia bays, forested valleys, bandstands with deckchair audiences wearing flat caps and berets. Who would say that in these early 1990s a respectable past didn't survive *somewhere*? On the stairs up to the cafe I had passed posters advertising 'Coming Attractions' in the Horizon Theatre itself, and these were just as passé and loveable. They featured popular performers of the 1960s and 1970s 'HERE SOON', such as the Melodreams, the Stitches in Time, also, surprisingly, a fair number of even older names still even now treading the boards because they knew no other life and needed the cash. These included 'the wonderful Nell Fraser', and Sid and Beryl Burgess and Company. *And Company*? I couldn't help wondering what size 'company' those particular dapper old pros now sustained, radio favourites of my father's not heard or seen via the airwaves for twenty years.

The café tables were glass-topped, the chairs made of painted cane, the wall lampshades were olive-green and singed by forty-watt bulbs. It was a dim, outdated place, and I liked it.

'I've written about when I was a child,' Rachel was saying. 'And a teenager.' (But how long had she not been a teenager?) 'There were these boys in school... But I haven't written about that.'

She laughed uncomfortably and scratched her ankle through the red socks she was wearing under rather smart tight-fitting trousers.

'I'd really like to read it if you wanted me to, 'I said. But after this burst of ambiguous revelation she was quiet and reserved, fidgeting with her empty coffee cup.

'Did you come here from work?' I asked, to find out what Rachel did and where she did it.

'I don't have work. I been looking for work. There isn't any in this place. I've got an A, a B, and a C, and I can't find any. I wouldn't have wanted to go to my third or fourth choice of university and they didn't want me at the first or second. I've just been reading and reading. And writing my book. All right, I *will* let you read it, no one else has.'

'Do you work on it while you're out?'

'I *never* work on it at home. I daren't. And I don't get any peace with my Mum or Dad. And my sister! And all her racket.'

'Racket?'

'Doesn't matter.'

'So you've been writing on the beach and in the country. But you can't write out of doors at this time of year, can you?'

'I do! I've been doing it all this afternoon in the shelter at the bus station. No one worries you, they're all wanting their buses.'

In this whole hour of coffee and low-level confidences Rachel had kept a distance, allowing me no physical openings. It was so different from my Polytechnic study, where an arm round the shoulder of someone distressed about losing a boyfriend, or doubting a husband, or getting a poor grade from a colleague, seemed friendly and natural, often producing a grateful response.

I had an idea. It needed to be proposed carefully.

'You'll have to stop writing outdoors when it gets really cold,' I remarked. 'I've got a table in a quiet room in my house where you...'

'I like it out of doors,' she said. It was not the first time in my life I had moved too fast. But I'd rarely regretted my folly so much.

'Let me see what you've written, anyway,' I tried.

I smiled and waited. I watched the slight shiftings of her shoulders as she pondered a decision, the uncertain smile, the uncrossing and re-crossing of the long legs.

'When can we next meet?'

Rachel shook her head, meaning she didn't know. My excitement faltered, my mode of resignation began to take hold. But she let me write down my address and phone number. Which I regretted immediately. Probably she would not call. There would be the long wait hoping that she might, and, when we next chanced to meet, embarrassment on either side.

But it was a small town. There would probably be a next chance encounter. I just wished I had left things to chance.

✳

I meant to put something on record, in case anyone reading here about Geoff Stedman thinks one tale that did the rounds of the Polytechnic was true. It was not true. It was, I think, put about by Dennis Frostick as a rather distasteful joke; and although Dennis would have been horrified to hear this, I believe it may have reached Management and done Geoff a certain amount of extra harm.

It was inspired by one of our 'fucking' conversations, which Dennis had overheard in the Drayhorse. Stedman was supposed to have gone to one of those periodic staff receptions when the humble lecturers were invited to meet Management and members of the Governing Council of the Polytechnic 'informally', over bad wine and canapés. We were all of us invited by rote, and I was not present but Geoff was. Thus I am not in a position categorically to deny that what follows actually happened, but I do not for a moment believe that it did.

The Director, Dr Tim Hulzer, and his wife Millicent were greeting guests as they arrived, at the door of the Maxwell Suite. Millicent Hulzer was wearing a dress with an especially low neckline, plenty of room for one of the necklaces she usually displayed, but on this occasion she had on a largish silver crucifix. The martyred Jesus lay flat and prominently on her talcumed skin above the trim, stitched border of the garment.

Having shaken hands first with Hulzer, Stedman is said to have moved on to his wife, shaken her hand warmly, dropped it, and looked closely at the ornament. He appeared to be thinking profoundly for many seconds, and then frowned, and sighed. Then he raised his hand again, and raised the crucifix from its position just above Mrs Hulzer's cleavage.

He is said to have looked at it long and thoughtfully, then shaken his head and placed it carefully back on the bare skin. And said, in a low voice, 'Fucking Romans!'

I do not consider that my friend Geoff Stedman would have done something so deplorable, and so counter to his interests in the Polytechnic, and I am glad to be able to deny the rumour that he ever did.

✳

Dear Rosie [I began],

I shall be at this address (I have no other special plans) up to and through Christmas and into the New Year. My days here are only too quiet and unremarkable. Nothing ever happens here [I have not seduced Rachel yet] *and I do assure you that boredom is my principal activity.*

Yours, Mike.

This, in late November, was in response to a further communication from Rosie, a letter which was a bit sharper than usual. She had written that although we had agreed we would only be in touch with the most basic information, my failure to contact her for several weeks was going too far. The tone was impatient, so I responded as above. She later told me that my 'November letter' confirmed her in the belief that I was undeniably available.

I posted it on a muggy, cloudy, damp Saturday at the very end of the month, having to go down to the post office because I had run out of stamps.

Flamingo, behind the glass partition, really was incredibly tall, tall enough for me to have to look up at her, a little. And she really did have a delicate, exotic-bird-like grace which entered all her movements: sliding forms and documents under the glass to her customers, tearing sheet of stamps along their perforation with slender but strong hands, neatly stamping receipts and postal orders. Rachel was more nervously lively in her movements but Flamingo had a powerful, unsmiling, dignified beauty that gave nothing away. I could not penetrate it. I tried.

Today. 'So what are these?' I asked when she pushed forward my stamps and my change with a captivating flourish of her fingers. The large stamps had an inscrutable seasonal design, a kind of Cubist bread-and-butter pudding in the middle of which an infant Jesus seemed to be waving a Christmas stocking (or condom?) at a corpulent robin. 'Can you put them on letters?'

'Special Christmas issue,' was all Flamingo said.

'In November? Is Christmas early this year?'

I gave a charming smile, spoke with a gentle deepening of my voice. But Flamingo did not answer, as if she sensed trouble. Or did not think my good humour worth responding to.

Some assistants in local shops were like this, taciturn, impassive, plain miserable. The ones you didn't want to make an impression on were often better. A girl in the chemist's next door, only there once so perhaps she was temporary, a sixth former earning pocket money, had served me with a small pair of scissors in long-ago August, smiling all the time, threading them onto her own finger and thumb in a quite unnecessary demonstration that was rather playful and provocative, or would have been if I had wanted to be provoked by her. Lastly she wrapped them too neatly in a paper bag, with little giggles, and handed them over with the words, 'There you go. Good snipping!' Flamingo never served licences or savings leaflets like that. Today I had looked for rapport and received a rebuff.

Her post office counter is, as I said, in Consumerama, biggest store in the High Street. Beside it a staircase takes you up to further levels, and at its foot they already had a red-robed, purple-faced, white-whiskered cardboard effigy: FATHER CHRISTMAS COMING SOON. I was tempted to go to the coffee shop at the top, but felt I needed something stronger when I had posted my letter to Rosie.

I'd heard rain suddenly falling while I was speaking to Flamingo. When I reached the entrance again a torrential downpour was going on, and there came a heavy growl of thunder. And I collided with Bill Bramston entering through the swing doors.

'Mike! How are you?' I sensed an unconvincing heartiness and a flicker of embarrassment in his voice and face when he saw me, cheerful and sheepish at the same time. There was also no need for the enquiry. I had been dropping in to see the Bramstons quite often. Jane had been phoning me quite often, as well. 'Hi, it's me,' she would say, and instantly she would be full of new photographic discoveries: the women had turned round and were walking towards the camera, the skirts were shorter, the attitudes more seductive. I had not been shown any yet, it was never quite convenient.

Bill and I walked back into the shop to talk and we ended up beside Santa Claus, where he stopped as if he had no purpose in coming here at all. For a few moments we stood in uneasy silence until I found the energy to bark, 'Well – cheers then, Bill' and wander off to the exit.

As I strode out into the downpour and dropped my terse letter to Rosie in the box outside, I happened to look up the street in the direction of the clifftop greens and saw the fork of lightning flash and zigzag down on the lighthouse tower like a contrived special effect in a film. I jumped in fright. Several people cried out. A couple screamed, and clutched each other. But all voices were drowned after two seconds by the huge crash and crack of thunder, bomblike, an instant of terror followed by an uprush of talk in the street, people running out of the rain faster, someone giving an incongruous laugh out of nervous relief. Then the rain was really hitting us, falling in solid lines, spurting inches high as it struck the floods in the gutters. I could only just elbow my way back through

46

Consumerama's glass doors among a band of similarly drenched and awestruck shoppers.

Away down the shop I could see Bill. For some reason I kept my eyes on him, tracking him along the wall displaying newspapers and journals just short of the greetings cards. When you see people you know at a distance, being themselves without your modification of their behaviour, they always look different. They can turn into odd strangers, which Bill was doing at this moment. He looked very furtive and suspicious.

He picked up a heavy Saturday edition of a broadsheet newspaper and added himself to a queue at a nearby till. He paid for the paper, but then he hung about next to the racks of popular magazines: DIY, computers, cookery, gardening, films.

A family around the cashier he had just left blocked Bill from my sight for a moment, probably from the cashier's sight as well. At that point Bill put out a rapid hand to a low shelf and picked up something which he slipped inside the voluminous pages of the newspaper. He walked in my direction quite slowly, unaware of me until he was very close. When he recovered from the shock of seeing me still there, 'Let's go, Mike,' he said firmly. He took me by the right arm and almost manhandled me out of the door into the rain. Then he suddenly commanded 'Wait!', as if he wanted to show he was in no hurry, so we stood still. Next, with even greater suddenness, he grunted 'Come on!' and pushed me forward quickly along the pavement. It had the effect of making me feel complicit in his shoplifting.

Inside the Old Soldier I felt obliged by someone's embarrassment, not for the first time recently, to offer that person a drink. In a melée of customers sheltering from the storm, Greg (once I had caught his eye) actually served me fast, Bill's double and a single for myself. Bill's newspaper, still folded on our table when I brought the drinks, looked very wet from our short scamper along the street.

'I haven't seen a paper today,' I said, and put out my hand to pick it up.

Bill's hand fell on mine. I held on to the damp mass of newsprint and he was saying, 'Don't worry' and grabbing a different corner with a free hand. This ended in a small tug-of-war in which a thickness of soggy paper became detached from the rest. When I had the bundle fully on my lap he leaned over and took several layers of dry material from inside it, and a magazine not published with the newspaper fell on the floor.

'*Photo-Image?*' I said, handing it back to him. 'I didn't know you were keen on photography, Bill.'

He grabbed the journal and shoved it behind his back on the chair he occupied.

'Three pounds eighty for that!' he said hoarsely.

✳

Next week the local paper was full of the freak storm that had flooded cellars in the lower-lying areas of the town. On into December the weather stayed variable and malicious. One day the sea and shore would look unnaturally clear and vibrant in cold sunshine, the next four days would hide everything in dank mists.

I braved every kind of weather, every likely spot in the town and around it, in the hope of again meeting Rachel, who of course had not phoned. Some of the time, though, I thought about Rosie, I had phases of that. To be frank about it, I missed her sexual company. I tried to walk off the frustration.

On a second occasion I happened to see, in the darkness of early evening, those curious flashes from the interior of the lighthouse, all the odder now because it was closed for urgent repairs after the lightning had struck it. It was one night when it was dry and calm enough to walk along the lonely seafront by the light of the lamps the Council kept on right through the hours of darkness, even in the winter. From passing ships, I thought, our esplanade would look like a distant string of phosphorescent beads.

When I had seen such seafronts, foreign ones, from ships on which I was myself travelling, they had been among the most haunting and evocative sights imaginable. At lonely restaurant tables beyond those far illuminations waited women with faces shaped and made enthralling by the stress of inscrutable passions. If only I could be going to join someone like that – Rachel? Flamingo? – in such a restaurant in this town. As far as restaurants went, here there was only Captain Pedro's, listed in the food guides, expensive enough to be nicknamed locally 'the Swish Fish'.

I had had nearly enough of this walk. I would finish where the lamps finished, turn round and go back and have a bath in the house, activating the antiquated water-heater to fill the ancient tub. A mist had come down and was getting to my lungs. I was tempted to sit in one of the green-painted shelters along this stretch to get my breath back, there were two more ahead before I reached the last lamp and my turning point.

I didn't make it.

Rachel was sitting in the penultimate shelter, well wrapped up, wearing thick trousers and a heavy woollen coat, woollen scarf round her head, eyes staring down at a notebook page, lighted by a pocket torch, on which she was rapidly and intently writing.

When she raised her head and saw me, it was as if I was expected. 'Sit down, talk in a minute,' she said, the words coming out almost curtly. Then she spoke other words, to herself as she wrote them. 'People have the wrong children, but the children can't tell them that.' She put an emphatic stop at the end of the sentence, and looked up. 'Sorry.' Smiled.

I sat down on the shelter seat. Not close, not far away either. With Rachel within reach, a finely calculated gap. I realised I should be extremely cold if I stayed here long. I was not as warmly-clothed for sitting still as Rachel was, and she was now writing more. And more.

Light from her torch rose to illuminate the wooden sides of the shelter when she now and again paused to think. I saw alongside her head a graffito: 'I fuck Tracey's fanny, signed [sic] Andy'. Beside it, more chivalrously, was a roughly-sketched heart pierced by an arrow.

It was probably unconnected with an actual passion. Lovers' secrets and confessions are no longer put on public record like that; and carving names on tree-trunks would feel environmentally irresponsible. When much younger, a teenager say, I would have been embarrassed and saddened to see such a worldly male crudity in these circumstances, my feelings being deeper and finer. I was no longer so sensitive, but I still rather hoped Rachel would not have noticed it; it confronted me uncomfortably with my own nature.

We had sat together for possibly ten minutes and I was shivering. Her writing was clear, but not readable for me without Dr Koning's glasses, and I could not pull those out of my shirt pocket just to pry into Rachel's growing manuscript.

I looked at her fingers as she wrote, sticking out of the holes in her woollen mittens. When she paused she would clamp one hand over the other and draw her arms in to her sides.

Once, when he did not know I could hear, I heard my father say to a man friend, 'Sex is ninety-nine per cent timing'. Suddenly I thought I could put my right hand over Rachel's two clasped hands, our first physical contact. Of course my hand was gloved, it was that much less intimate a gesture. I am glad I didn't say something like 'Rachel' at that moment, let alone use an endearment. I just suggested, after a few seconds, 'What about a warmer place?' I withdrew my hand as I spoke, as an earnest of perfectly proper intentions.

As we entered the Old Soldier, Greg sent across the bar the iciest and most contemptuous look I had ever had from him. The bristles of his black beard seemed to stiffen and freeze, the black eyes bored into us, his chest under the black nautical sweater heaved with hostility.

Rachel went with me to the bar and appeared to be trying to soften Greg's image of aggression with a relaxed smile. I asked her what she wanted. 'Big Bloody Mary. And some crisps, please.' By this time Greg's back was unalterably turned on us. I tried a wholly unironic cough, a non-committal throat-clearing. He did not move. 'Hullo, Greg,' Rachel said. Greg turned, and looked for

50

someone else to serve. His bad luck; there was no one. I ordered, pleasantly enough, I thought. He said nothing, peering with hatred at the very glasses and optics he was handling for us.

He put the drinks down near to his side of the wide counter, where I had to stretch out my arm fully to reach them. He slapped down my change on the same spot. As I collected it, I imagined a knife pinning my hand to the bar. Greg looked hard at Rachel, then back at me, significantly, and turned away again. Only then did I realise that Rachel had used his name.

She drank and ate as if she was famished, but also wanted to get away fast; whereas I wanted to keep the meeting going, build on her renewed willingness to let me treat her, to the third large drink I had bought for someone in an uneasy atmosphere.

I wanted to know how she knew Greg, but she spoke first.

'Didn't know *he* worked here,' she said.

'Do you know him?'

'No. I know *about* him, though.'

I didn't think Greg could hear us, but he was looking in our direction again. Having glanced up at him when I spoke I thought it best not to continue on this theme.

'How much more have you written?' I asked.

'Listen,' she said after a pause, clutching the notebook as if I might seize it from her. 'I *will* show you some of what I've written. The beginning parts.' She drained her glass, but foresaw that I might offer her another and went straight on. 'But not now. I don't have those parts with me. Soon.'

'Any time you wish. '

'It was... quite hard to decide to let anyone see it, but it was nice you wanted to. I've been copying out some so you could have it to read for an idea of it. It's been very painful writing this, but I've had to. What about Friday? Friday *week*, I mean?'

'To meet, you mean? *Yes*.'

'I've got to be somewhere that night. The theatre. We could meet there. I could bring it.'

Outside again, she refused the courtesy of my escorting her even

51

part of the way home. 'Right, then. By the box office at 7.15 Friday week.'

'See you.'

Rachel was proposing to pass on her manuscripts if we went on that night to see Sid and Beryl Burgess. And Company.

✳

I deserved to be ejected from the Polytechnic much sooner than Geoff Stedman, and with good reason. But I lasted beyond him. In effect I was 'fired' not long after he was, but in fact it was simply suggested to me that in view of certain complaints about me an early retirement might be arranged to avoid problems.

Dennis Frostick got it right, I think, during a four-hour academic meeting which I had said was 'going to kill me', when he started to write my *Times* obituary, for use if my death actually occurred.

> '*The death of Mike Barron removes one of the most zealous and experienced womanisers of his, or any other, generation.*
>
> *If an early childhood fascination with current affairs came to eventual fruition in his appointment as Lecturer in Politics and Auxiliary Modules at —— Polytechnic, that aptitude was frequently outpaced by his talent and fervour in the pursuit of female schoolmates, the older girls (though this preference, if never entirely absent, was to feature less prominently in later years) offering him more scope than the younger.*
>
> *The arrival of puberty hugely enhanced Barron's enthusiasm and sharpened his abilities. As with so many men of achievement, he always acknowledged his debt to his teachers, though to the end he remained reticent about the influence of one in particular, cited in his autobiography* Going It Together *as "Miss Bellamy". On this pseudonymous mentor he lavished much grateful praise for her part in his education.*

52

Arriving as one of the first male students to be admitted to the formerly all-female —— College in the University of London, Barron won immediate respect for his thoroughness in promoting popular extra-curricular activities...'

And so on. But insofar as my behaviour justified Frostick's tribute, I am bound to say that I ended up not proud of it. During my autumn and winter months in this town I had felt the lack of opportunities acutely. But I also experienced some shame about seizing them in the past. I would never have entered on the agreement with Rosie if I hadn't thought I might settle down.

Stedman never referred to these tendencies of mine, though he must have known of (most of) them. He was never, absolutely never, guilty of such things himself. Stedman was only ever the impeccable, devoted teacher. Which was what made his dismissal so unjust.

I remember when I first became convinced that Dave Underhill was moving decisively against Geoff. Faithful to his promise, Geoff had reported the rising water on the Games Field to Torridge, out of courtesy copying his memo to Dave Underhill as his departmental boss. Perhaps Underhill interpreted this as an arcane method of seeking favour; at any event the action was deliberately resented, Dave becoming all the more impatient with him. Through some devious reassessment of student numbers it seemed likely that someone would have to go, and Dave made sure that Geoff came top of the list.

I had seen that little man do something I had never managed, perhaps because teaching politics in the Thatcher-Major-Kinnock era didn't lend itself to it: come out of a class drained and elated, very occasionally weeping as well. Not with *playing* Hamlet or Lear but from interpreting them. He could be shaking and speechless – a striking condition in his case – from pure passion after taking students through passages of *Middlemarch* or *Anna Karenina*, or poems by Hopkins or Hardy. 'When I get desperate about them understanding these things,' he said one day (I'd put an arm round him to calm him down because he had no fags left and the next

53

drink was an hour away) 'how can I be serious about the likes of Dave Underhill?'

It was the final pre-Christmas lunch at the Polytechnic, in the long echoing second-floor refectory shared by staff and students. There was some bad wine at our table, donated by Underhill and therefore the ignorant choice of a man who preferred a joint to a jar. A sense of uneasy jollification blanketed the company. We had crackers, bought by Kathy Feltham (now there was an older woman I had a lot of time for), so we had to pull them, read out the riddles, put on the paper hats. When all that was over we all went up a bit mournfully in the lift to a badly-timed last meeting of term in Dave's fourth floor study.

Dave kept his radio playing throughout the day, whatever was happening in his room. Today was what Stedman (who thought it a bad sign) called 'a right ear day.' In his forties, ever conscious of cultural trends, Dave had taken to earrings; each of his large ears was double-pierced. Mostly he wore just one ring in each ear, but sometimes he had both in one ear and today it was the right ear.

He spread himself with feigned informality over an easy chair in front of his desk while we, the English and auxiliary specialists in his department, sat on uncomfortable plastic seats. Round the wall, a collection of pop posters, old or recent, scowled or simpered at the proceedings, and behind Underhill a computer screen repeated and repeated a coloured flurry of migraine-inducing graphics.

All we had to do was settle some minor matter of teaching assignments following the arrival, in January, of a new lecturer to replace the worthy old Roy McCullum, who had taken early retirement because of illness. It was known (Stedman certainly knew) that although Roy's successor had been appointed with the usual procedures, he was very much to Underhill's liking, known to Dave already, in effect a personal appointee.

Dave read in a rapid laid-back manner from an A4 sheet of jottings. His designer casualness irritated Stedman, who fidgeted. Behind Underhill's throwaway cadences the radio added a low, rhythmic thudding to the background of tension in the room.

'Nick will have CM2 for next term's AM to replace Roy,' Dave was saying. CM2 was a group in Catering Management's second year and their AM (Auxilary Module) for the term had usually been an undemanding but valuable 'humanities' course called 'Classics of Modern Fiction.'

'Who is "Nick"?' Stedman asked sharply.

I did not like the sound of this. Kathy Feltham thought she could defuse the situation by whispering the name in Geoff's ear. She was wrong. Besides, Geoff knew the answer and was merely requiring Underhill to have the courtesy to tell us formally about a new colleague.

'Nick Jackson, Roy's replacement,' Dave replied, in an impatient drawl.

'Didn't catch the name,' Stedman complained, head down and trying to write it. It made Dave feel foolish for having to repeat it.

'What will he do with CM2?'

'Film Studies.'

This change had not been mentioned before, and I was surprised. Underhill was trying to get away with a shift in the content of the Module which he had the power to arrange but which might have been referred to a course planning subcommittee first.

'*Film* Studies?'

'He'll be looking at early rock movies with them.'

This was far away on the other side of Stedman's boundary line, well outside his palisade.

'Ha!'

It was not a loud ejaculation, but this contemptuous monosyllable of Geoff's was familiar to me and no doubt to Dave Underhill also. The air filled with static. I tried to pretend I wasn't listening. I tried looking down the gullet of a screaming head on one of Dave's posters, but it didn't work.

'Is there a rock movie of *The Golden Bowl*?' Stedman asked quietly. The Henry James novel had been one of Roy McCullum's classic fiction choices, and Underhill would have known that. He looked at Geoff and fingered his unembellished left ear.

'Geoff,' he drawled slowly, making the activity comprised in his final word sound remote and repellent, 'even you can't pretend that CM2 want to *read*.'

I sensed at that moment that Dave Underhill and 'Management' would have plans for Geoff Stedman's future.

✳

Brutal and vindictive were the words for what the weather became now, four days before I was due to go to the show in the Horizon Theatre with Rachel. The sea was sluggish but the winds from inland ripped branches off trees in the gardens and the High Street was a funnel for the blast. If you stood with your back to it, it pushed you forward, it threatened to topple you over if you faced it. Any rubbish on the ground was fiercely propelled at you, any dropped object blown away. A dog-owner must have heard her pet's appeal to 'do his stuff', but when she set the tiny quadruped down, he or she had to scrabble with all four paws to be able to stand still and foul the pavement.

Letting the wind take me towards Consumerama and Flamingo (vainly, as it turned out), I found myself suddenly up against a small, solid figure widening its arms to halt me. In case I was blown over, I thought, but the gesture was not as sociable as that and the arms were Trevor Ridyard's.

'What *you* up to, then?' With a derisive stress on the 'you'. This time he was in blue corduroy trousers, a dirty donkey jacket, a little black plastic rain hat with holes in its sides (it was not raining). He had pulled it down to the level of his eyebrows and his eyes peered out from under it like the eyes of a stage comedian seeking to raise a laugh with his first glance at the audience. That was not Trevor's intention.

'I'm "up" to some shopping.'

Suddenly I noticed Jane coming out of the door of the chemist's opposite, like last time (the first and only time I'd met Ridyard, to whom I now seemed very familiar?) unusual for a time of day when she might be fully occupied at the hotel. I was about to wave to her when Ridyard punched me. In what others might have seen as a jovial gesture, but quite hard. In the chest. 'Keeping yourself busy, then?' No smile, no pleasantness, a challenge. Jane walked slowly up the street behind me and Trevor seemed to be following her with his eyes, at the same time wishing to keep me talking.

And next, another strange circumstance: Flamingo was emerging from the swing doors of Consumerama (I saw her over Trevor's shoulder) followed by Greg, who was talking and gesticulating. The wind lifted and billowed the back of an old raincoat he had on, and Flamingo strode rapidly ahead as if she had no wish to stop or listen. In the blast she made easy progress, like a lavish and refined bird sure of the air currents, repeatedly shaking her head. Distracted by this sight, I failed to hear what Ridyard was asking me until he shouted it.

'I said, "You go round the Bramstons' most days"?'

'I'm there some days, yes.'

He did not look convinced.

'You going there *Christmas*?'

I had no notion at all of what I would do at Christmas, and said so. I had been going to Flamingo's post office to buy stamps again, one for a card for Rosie in which I would make sure she knew we could not bend our agreement to meet at the festive season; a pre-emptive message.

'Might see you there if you are,' Trevor said. From under the rain hat he looked at me hard and uncomically for several seconds, then said 'Ciao!' abruptly and walked away past me.

Jane had walked off in the direction of her home. It would be warm there for a few minutes, I thought, and I felt like telling her what I had not been able to yet, about Bill and the photography magazine; also asking if she could explain Trevor Ridyard's behaviour.

But when I battled my way back against the wind and rounded

her nearby corner I found I was following Ridyard. I slowed up. What if he was...? I would have to walk on past Jane's gate when I reached it. Except that, just before the gate, Trevor turned round, saw me, and carried on. He was head down against the hurricane and negotiating the next intersection as I dared to ring Jane's bell.

Her door opened at once, but only a chink. 'Mike!' she said with surprise. Then she opened it widely. But in the second before, her face had been showing not surprise but another reaction.

'Saw you in the High Street. I thought I might catch you in.'

'Yes, I – I came back for a bit of lunch.'

'You don't lunch at work?'

'Not – not every day. Would you like something?' Awkwardly.

I accepted with trepidation; she was putting home-made rolls on the table. Never mind, the shop cheese looked all right. To eat it, we sat on stools in the kitchen, looking out at the wind lashing the garden.

'I had a peculiar encounter with your friend Trevor Ridyard just now.'

'Oh really?'

'And I've been wanting to tell you about when I met Bill in the storm last Saturday week.'

I described the confrontation with Trevor first.

'Why should he be so aggressive?'

'You ought to meet him properly. He's not like that when you know him.'

Then her telephone rang. Out in the dim hall Jane had a long muffled conversation with someone. I was staring at the garden and seeing that the wind had blown open the shed door. Bill's old blue bicycle stood inside.

She was not going to tell me about the phone call, so I said, nodding in the direction of the shed,

'I thought Bill had sold his old bike.'

'Oh – he kept it.'

'Does he use it? Only, a few months ago I thought I saw it. It was where Dibdin Street crosses the main road...'

58

'There must be someone else's like his,' Jane cut in. Too quickly.
'Does Bill buy photographic magazines?'
'Not that I know of.'
'Only... he was acquiring one when we met in Consumerama the other day. Not buying one, but acquiring it.'
I told her all the detail of the incident.
Photo-Image? He must be hiding that as well. I haven't seen it. I've been seeing a lot of new snaps, though. He's got a camera with a zoom now. The girls are getting closer. Sometimes it's only parts of the girls.'
'Are they any particular girls? Are they repeating?'
'A few crop up several times. But there are new ones all the time. It's got to be an obsession, there are *hundreds* now.'
Part of my memory of Jane at the Polytechnic was that she propped herself up with fantasy at times of stress: fantasies of hope, of persecution bravely resisted, ordinary amatory fantasies. So I pressed her on these photographs.
'You are certain there's no one you recognise? From around the town?'
'*No*! I'd know them if there were. And I'd know the locations. The beaches might be anywhere, of course. No, everybody knows everyone and everything here, you can't avoid it.'
Yes. I knew Greg, and Flamingo. Greg knew Flamingo, it seemed. Bill, Jane, Trevor Ridyard and I knew each other. I knew Rachel. Rachel knew Greg's name. *Who else knew Rachel?* I didn't think Jane and Bill did, but I didn't care to enquire. I wouldn't want Jane to see me and Rachel together...
'Can you let me see some?'
She appeared to consider that for a moment. Appeared to. 'Yes. But... not now. I've got to be back. Some time you can see them.'
'Jane,' I said, 'you can always tell me about all of these things – at *any* time, please. You know me. But we've got to talk about it properly.'
'I do know you, Mike. Yes, we *will* talk about it.'
We were standing by the door, and suddenly she half-sobbed, a

small, catching, mild moaning sound. She turned and put her arms round me, kissed me, and went on kissing when I responded. Then she patted my cheek, brightened her face into a courageous smile, and opened the door onto the tumult.

※

My seasonal card crossed with one from Rosie. It had her written greetings (rather too warmly expressed) but mainly consisted of a new photograph; we had not said anything about photographs when we established our rules for the year. I stood this picture with a card from the Bramstons and one from Dennis Frostick on the mantelpiece in my appalling 'dining-room' and thus saw the full-length Rosie every day, a strongish reminder.

I realised I missed Rosie. As I have hinted, it was a sexual loss, although I also missed someone to tell about Bill and Jane (up to a point, of course), and Greg, and Trevor. Once I came in late from the new pub I had discovered (Greg had made the Old Soldier a virtual no-go area) and caught myself blowing a kiss at the photograph with the third and fourth fingers of a hand. And that wouldn't do at all. I had to think harder, more systematically, less frivolously about my future.

All the same, the angle from which the photographer (who was that?) had taken the snap showed that Rosie was still an attractive example of Air Hostess's Leg.

Sufferers from this syndrome can be spotted all the time if you stand and watch air crew women coming off duty in any major airport in the world. They have lengthened thighs and shortened lower legs, the latter sometimes reduced to forty per cent or less of the full limb. It happens to them as a consequence of their spending hours of every working day trying to stand or walk steadily and calmly in the aisle of an aircraft in flight. The constant pressure on the knees pushes them down inches below their normal position, towards the feet. This condition, not harmful to suffer from but familiar to orthopaedic specialists, is aggravated if, for any reason of emergency, the sufferer has to walk uphill along the aisle when a plane is climbing or downhill when it is descending, a time when air crew are normally keeping to their seats.

I find the affliction very seductive.

My new pub, oddly called the Constant Hope, lay on the inland outskirts of the town, a spacious and rather impersonal hostelry with a restaurant and 'music bar' attached. I had been noticing the advertised attractions, and the day after my lunchtime visit to Jane I decided to take a look at the jazz evening featured on their notices. It was late, but I would give it a try.

I knew with a sudden pang of regret that I had known very little entertainment in this town. I felt it very strongly when I pushed open a heavy front door and heard with a glow of pleasure the sound of the musicians in full spate. How little it takes to make you feel a little happier and distract you from your other preoccupations... As I ordered, I stood listening and made out a piano, a tenor sax, a bass, percussion. 'Satin Doll' was what they were playing, and at this hour the fast variations they were improvising were likely to be the final item. The posters said they were the *Vic Tillinghurst Quartet*.

I carried my glass through to where about twenty enthusiasts sat at tables listening, greeting solos with due volleys of applause. I saw Vic's young pianist working a respectable grand piano, took in an older bass player outlined against a back wall, watched Vic himself, on saxophone, prominent and commanding downstage on the little platform, urging his sidesmen on ever faster through his speeded-up rendering of the suave old Ellington number.

My back was turned to the quartet for a few moments as I put down my drink, shed my hat, coat and scarf, and dropped them on a vacant chair. Only when I sat down and faced the musicians again did I focus the fourth of them among a shining collection of drums, cymbals and high-hats: Flamingo.

At that second she sat virtually still. Statuesque without posing. Giving just a regular crisp tap with her drumstick on the rim

61

of her snare drum. With impassive face, eyes gazing out neutrally over the small audience. Her legs were stretched out at full length to her left. By her right shoulder was a microphone into which she could have sung. Did Flamingo sing? That wasn't the whole surprise either. Vic finished a solo, nodded at a small clatter of clapping, listened through some decent flourishes from his pianist, smiled at some gloomy, introverted thudding from the bass, led the quartet into a snappy reprise of the refrain and ended it with some cheerfully discordant send-up extravagances. Everything was brought to an absolutely final close with a few seconds of wild energy from Flamingo, whirling herself around her percussion department. 'Yeah!' called out somebody at the back.

Flamingo then laid down her sticks and swivelled the mike round to her lips, which were saying, 'Thank you – thank you – Satin Doll, Satin Doll, Satin *Doll*. We are – but you knew already, I hope – the Vic Tillinghurst Quartet. That's Nige Loveday on bass – John Stainer on piano – Tony Crowther on tenor sax –' all this slowed up by patters of ritual applause '– and over here on the hardware I am Victoria Tillinghurst.'

People were rising from their seats, the band was recovering its breath. One of the seated listeners was making his way, against the tide, up between the tables to the front. Greg had reached the front before the bass player, not as big as Greg but as burly as his instrument, rested it against his chair and stepped down to confront him. He did this by barring Greg's path towards Flamingo and opening his arms wide.

I heard what he said. It was words of welcome. Nige Loveday was saying, 'Hi Greg, come on lad, have one on me! What's it to be, Greg?' Flamingo darted a look at the two of them but mainly preferred not to notice. 'Easy on, old son,' Nige said; and was winning, because any scene would have to be started by Greg against this show of warmth, and he didn't seem to relish the embarrassment. 'It's *my* turn, Greg. It's my *pleasure*. Come on, lad.'

At this point, but only then, Greg saw me, as he was coaxed or ushered towards the bar. The expression on his face changed from deep discomfort to black suspicion and patent rage. It came to me that if he was here in this pub, then he could not be at his own bar in the Old Soldier to-night and how was that? I had never been there without seeing him.

I stood still. Flamingo began to load her drums into big boxes. When Greg had gone, I went over, unimpeded.

'This is great. Thank you,' I told her.

'Well thank yoo–!' Flamingo drawled with a practised smile, showing no sign of knowing who I was. I suppose I hung about just a little too long after that, because she smiled again, emphatically, and said, to dismiss me, 'See you later.'

✳

This was awful. On the Friday afternoon I had taken a bath so as to look and smell my best for an evening beside her in a warm theatre, and while cooling off had fallen asleep in one of the cavernous and grubby lounge armchairs in front of the electric fire. I had also dreamt of Rosie, something about Air Hostess thighs activating an X-ray portal at Stansted...

I'd intended to stroll down early, assembling my thoughts about my prospects with Rachel as I went. But as it was now late, I had to drive down, at speed, arriving with only a minute to spare. I had purchased two tickets on the edge of a small side row of seats, thinking we might be more private. But in the foyer Rachel was waiting for me with two of her own in her hand (holding in the other a Consumerama plastic bag). It shamed me.

'You've paid for these already?'

'They're comps,' Rachel said, motioning me towards the entrance. '*Complimentaries.*'

We entered the small, worse-for-wear auditorium circumspectly, passing the poster suggesting we 'Get in the mood for the festive season with SID AND BERYL BURGESS: A SONG, A DANCE, A SMILE.' It was not warm but vaguely chilly, the arms of the seats cold to the touch. Very quiet background muzak came over on a tape that occasionally jumped. No doubt to save energy, few of the house lights were on, so it was hard to tell whether I might recognise any of the twelve or so other persons scattered across the stalls. Rachel rested her plastic bag on the empty seat beside her. There were hardly twenty of us when, several minutes late, the muzak stopped and live music (piano and drums) struck up in the orchestra pit.

I wished I could have picked my parents' brains for information about Sid and Beryl. My father would have remembered their names. My mother, who was the political activist in the household (I had gravely disappointed her by becoming just a lecturer in Politics instead of a member of parliament) – my mother could have recalled and placed their kind of entertainment. On the wide and intricate social scale of comedians they stood, I seemed to think, not for the resilient working class, Cockney or Lancashire, nor for the suave-suited troupers who worked on the fringe of cabaret or in the genteel English musical. The Burgesses were the archetypally bland and amiable, happy middle-class couple whose 'light comedy' would offend no one and appeal to any undemanding audience in any place except the rowdiest halls. My oldest readers might like to think of them as a Jack Hulbert and Cicely Courtneidge with rougher edges.

They had long fallen off the TV screen, where they had not been very comfortable, and there was no route back to the radio given their age and the advent, in the later 1980s, of young 'alternative' comedians. 'Stars of Stage, Radio, TV and Film', their publicity went on (what film, and when?)

Onstage, when the curtains pulled jerkily apart, were their 'company', an advance guard of three persons and a wire-haired terrier. The dog took up a sitting position downstage under its own spotlight while the humans went into a dance routine. Two, announced later as 'our very own youngsters, Dick and Cindy', were unusually young by comparison with Sid and Beryl. The third company member, 'Nobby', was older, tattier, in a tight-fitting, well-worn striped suit, chirpy and agile but looking exactly like a down-on-his-luck performer who had somehow gravitated to this show.

When Sid and Beryl appeared, entering from opposite wings after three minutes' warming up by this trio, only Rachel clapped; the rest of the tiny audience was too slow to give them any hoped-for celebrity applause. The 'stars' gazed out warmly into every corner as if playing to a full house. I felt sad with embarrassment, almost sick with sadness. The proceedings were terrible, though I admired those people up there with something near to tears of sympathy for their carrying on as if nothing had changed in the world. They had inextinguishable nerve to keep it all up. When they died, few living persons would remember them and they would get only a couple of obituary sentences in the theatre journals.

I dislike dogs, but had to give Nobby's terrier credit. Nobby did a juggling turn, conducted a bit of backchat with a non-existent audience member, found a flea in the ticket pocket of his jacket and told it an Irish joke, whistled up the animal. 'Chris' walked up one side of a see-saw plank, barked three times at the top, trotted neatly down the other side, jumped easily through hoops with which Nobby tried to confuse him, ran adroitly between Nobby's legs while he did exercises, leapt onto a high stool handed out to him from the wings and from there jumped onto Nobby's broad head where he balanced for several seconds while the drum rolled in the pit.

The Burgesses did a quick-fire middle-aged-man-and-wife-at-the-seaside sketch, and the lights came up for the interval. Rachel put the plastic bag in my hand.

'This it?' I asked.

'It.'

'Do you want to come back after the interval?' I would go anywhere rather than stay for further passages of pathos on that stage, now that I had Rachel's writings safely in my hand.

'Of course,' she replied.

'You wouldn't prefer to go?'

'*No!*'

'What about the tickets? You can't treat me.'

'I told you – they were comps. My Mum got them.'

'Your mother did?'

'On the piano.'

The two persons on piano and drums in the pit, both women, were standing up. So the older one was Rachel's mother. And naturally, by the rule that so many things were surprising that surprise itself was becoming unsurprising, the drummer was Flamingo. As we passed she caught sight of me, and looked.

When I looked back she nodded at me, with clear recognition. After feeling excited by that, I felt caught out. By Rachel's wondering how I knew the drummer? Or by Flamingo seeing me with Rachel? Rachel nodded at Flamingo, to add her own greeting to mine, I supposed. We went out for a drink in the silent and deserted bar.

In the second half, after another spell of dancing, Sid and Beryl Burgess talked to each other across the stage on two telephones, busy husband in the office called by his wife on a bad line about a plumbing problem. At last there was laughter from the audience, possibly people remembering an old sketch. Cindy and Dick sang, a passable romantic ballad, and then came a schoolroom scene in which Sid put on glasses and mortar board to teach sums to the rest, Beryl a naughty girl in front, Nobby in short trousers regularly interrupting from the back. Then Nobby stripped down to vest and underpants to take a bow and arrow as Cupid for some stand-up comedy. Dick and Cindy reappeared in lime green light as Harlequin and Columbine, a serious bit of ballet which, because it was 'sad', did gain some genuine applause. How much longer could I bear this?

Ultimately Sid appeared in front of the curtain while objects were being moved around behind it and thanked us for being so nice to meet. If we had friends in Cromer, or Mablethorpe, or Llandudno, we were to let them know they'd be coming there on their New Year tour. He hoped to see us all again here, when they came back – 'maybe a few more of you?' – but seriously we had been a lovely audience and ours was a lovely town. He'd like to settle down one day in a place like this, perhaps he and Beryl would actually do that. But the busy life of touring entertainers still called...

Meanwhile, then, he wished us all a Merry Christmas, a Happy New Year, and to end the show tonight –

The curtains parted for a climactic turn which even I recalled – could it be from a live variety show in my childhood? It involved the entire troupe again. Sid Burgess was a posh, endlessly patient men's and women's outfitter. He had to cope with Beryl as a scatty, never-satisfied South Kensington customer, Dick and Cindy as two stylish youngsters in search of fashions he didn't stock, and Nobby as an ordinary working-class bloke who had strayed into the wrong shop. The dog, belonging to the lady, interfered with every transaction, getting under people's feet, barking, begging.

Without thinking I began to laugh at the changes and flauntings of unsuitable garments (Nobby in a brassière), the ancient slang, the timing perfected in a thousand repetitions. I was glad, because I did want the Burgesses to go home happy. I hoped they were receiving a decent fixed fee, not a percentage of box office takings.

Everyone came together in a row for the final song-and-dance, and yes, I recalled their signature tune, which Rachel's mother thumped out on the piano with energy and no doubt relief:

> Sleep well – and wake up to sunshine –
> There's sunshine – to-morrow – for you!

The curtains closed for good and all. Until their second and final performance to-morrow.

'Do you want to say hullo to your Mum?' I asked Rachel. If she didn't, I would propose another drink in the theatre bar.

'I'll do that at home,' she said. 'She'll be pleased I've dragged someone along to support her – and my sister will.'

'Your sister?'

'On the drums.'

✳

Through the autumn I had known the slow unseen drift of purposeless days, giving me late November when September was only just ending. But, love or despise them, the fixed points of the year at least interrupted and punctuated that invisible process.

It was the brink of Christmas now. I was in Consumerama. Let's describe it a little more. As I've said, the Ground Floor has newspapers and magazines, and Flamingo's post office. There are also sweets and chocolates and jigsaw puzzles, cards 'for all occasions', stationery, a few shelves of popular paperbacks. On the First Floor is a wide room offering a range of men's and women's clothes, and at one end a sizeable toys department. Upstairs from that, you could find jewellery, cosmetics, sports gear and so on, and a Coffee Room.

There is a lift, but four days before Christmas I was ascending to the First Floor by the stairs thinking I might look at some trousers, when I met Flamingo – I *must* try to call her 'Victoria' – coming down. She didn't notice me. Or I assumed so.

On the First Floor I strolled idly from display to display looking at Winter garments which might soon be reduced in a post-Christmas sale; the Summerwear end having long been cleared for the installation, next to Toys, of Santa's Magic Train and Polar Palace.

If it was like what I recalled from early childhood you entered the Train through a small door, sat down in a First Class compartment, and watched a moonlit panorama of snow, turreted castles and reindeer-drawn sledges pass by on a revolving tableau, as engine noise and mysterious music came through a loudspeaker. You covered vast and magic distances. When you finally arrived in the Polar Palace you alighted from the compartment by its opposite door and met Father Christmas, white-bearded and God-like on a glistening silver throne. You had to vow to be good, and you could then dip into his sack and take out a gift. I remembered all this from the local Royal Arsenal Co-operative Society store in Plumstead.

Today in Consumerama I was reflecting on how remote my innocent infancy was, and how different from that awarded me in Dennis Frostick's obituary. I had never really understood my childhood: my father's unexplained absences, my mother's hours spent addressing piles of election envelopes. And yet I felt very close to it in spirit, even after all the time that had invisibly and pointlessly vanished. I longed to dip my hand down into a sack of promise offered by some generous and wise being, and take out of it a key to open and explain everything.

For a moment today I felt as bewildered and vulnerable as a child. The child's tears could easily have run down the furrows of the face of the old man trying without Dr Koning's spectacles to read the sizes of the trousers on the display racks.

It increased the poignancy of my mood when I saw that Consumerama's Santa had left his Polar Palace for the moment, perhaps for lack of children to reward for their professions of goodness, and was standing at his door looking across the clothes displays. In my direction. His fluffy-bearded features looked troubled and sad, I thought. Was he, also, musing on childhood, time and innocence? I went on looking at the trousers on the stands.

But when I looked up again Father Christmas was striding down the floor of the shop towards me.

When he reached me I stood aside to let him pass. But he did not pass. He stopped. And we were face-to-face. And he addressed me. Before his words came out there was a considerable twitching of the white beard, and a scowl I recognised.

'Piss off, you lecherous old bastard,' Greg was shouting.

'What?' I said. Or thought I said. I was too shocked to know whether I had in fact spoken the word.

'You heard me – Piss off!'

You don't stop to find out the reasons for hostility of this kind from someone younger and stronger than you. But I kept enough dignity not to move away in haste, merely turning and retreating with a quiet, 'I see.'

At the top of the stairs I felt a hand applied between my shoulderblades with some force. Not enough to overbalance me, but I had to grab at the banister.

'And fucking *keep* away! Understand?' Greg called out as I

descended. Coming up at the same time were two mothers with small children. One said, 'Oh look, Santa Claus has come to meet us.'

At Christmas I told Jane about this incident, because inexplicable dislike disturbs me. Apparently the Assistant Manageress, or 'AM', in charge of that floor had noticed Greg's trips down to the post office in his Santa Claus disguise, and seen how he had come out of his Polar Palace when Flamingo had dared to come upstairs to look at some clothes that lunchtime. Something had passed between them, and Flamingo had left quickly – then Greg had behaved violently towards me and she had to take her own life in her hands and confront him, worried for the reputation of the store.

This AM was called Anne, and she knew Jane well, also apparently recognised me without knowing I knew Jane. Anne's description of an 'elderly tall man, practically bald, in an old-fashioned raincoat' suggested to Jane that it might be me, but she wasn't going to mention it to me herself.

When Greg, trembling with aggression, had calmed down enough to explain, he told the AM that I was a local menace who needed talking to, or more. He had seen me, whoever I was, pestering several young women hereabouts. Not only in the Old Soldier pub, where he used to work, but at the post office downstairs, and in the street, and in the Co-op superstore in the outskirts, and elsewhere. I was about to dismiss all this as paranoid suspicion when Jane said that sadly, yes, I had gained a name locally for talking to shop assistants and eyeing them up. I was known for rolling grapefruit and oranges down the counter to raise a smile from girls at the Co-op checkouts. In the bank I was regarded as 'a bit of an old Romeo'.

As for Greg, Jane had learnt from Anne in Consumerama that he had separated from his wife, who had taken her children to live in Jesmond, near Newcastle-on-Tyne while he was in his last year in the Royal Navy. On his discharge, the only work he could immediately find as a stopgap here, in his home town, in a time of acute unemployment, was the barman's job in the Old Soldier, a pub only prospering in the summer season. The sympathetic landlord had kept him on well beyond the summer, but three weeks ago he had to be laid off. At just that moment the regular, veteran Santa Claus at Consumerama went down with a stroke, and Greg had stepped into his boots. The work paid him, but made him all the more morose because he missed his own children and had to sit offering gifts to other people's.

Shortly after starting at the Old Soldier Greg had fallen abjectly in love with a local shopgirl (Jane didn't connect this with 'Flamingo', or Victoria, and I didn't tell her.) The girl was not interested, so Greg began, in effect, to stalk her. He was said very recently to have been forcibly removed from another local pub where he had found her with other men friends; my theory was that the incident I witnessed at the Constant Hope had been exaggerated into this. So, when Greg saw me in Consumerama just after he had spotted Flamingo examining the displays outside his grotto...

'Do I really have a reputation?' I asked.

'Yes. Old habits die hard, don't they!'

Of course I spent some of Christmas Day at the Bramstons', roughly mid-afternoon until moderately late in the evening. There had been an open invitation; I could go if I wanted to, but if I had other plans they would not expect me. Rosie was with her mother, so I didn't even need to wonder if I should break our pledge and phone to wish her well. Again and again in a lonely morning I ended up in front of her card on the mantelpiece, picking it up, putting it down again, turning it round so that I couldn't see her air hostess pose, turning it back again. No, I knew I couldn't spend the rest of the day in this house by myself.

At Bill and Jane's we were, unexpectedly, seven in number: Jane and Bill, Zilla and Rory, Trevor Ridyard I'm afraid, who made no attempt to speak to me at all after a nod of surly greeting, myself – and Treazy.

Treazy ('Easy Treazy' as twelve-year old Rory afterwards named her) was a young friend of Zilla's, the same age. If there *was* any pleasure in the day it was due to her, although Zilla also was more sociable in her company. Treazy conversed very maturely for her years, asked questions and thought about the answers, helped with the food, was generally well-mannered and engaging. When she and Zilla retired to a bedroom to watch a video she had brought, I asked Jane, was she a friend from school?

Jane laughed. 'Yes, but it's a "teenager adoption scheme".'

'What do you mean?'

Last Christmas Zilla had been so bored and unco-operative that the day had been a horror. But Bill had noticed that teenage friends Zilla brought home were mostly polite, charming, altogether tolerable. So Jane spoke to parents who came into her hotel bar, had similar accounts of awkward Christmases, and came up with an exchange operation. They 'adopted' Treazy, who behaved impossibly at home, for Christmas, and Zilla would go to Treazy's parents for New Year, neither girl yet being of an age to be permitted just to spend either festival with peers.

Treazy found out something I had been unable to. For a game, we all played one I remembered from long-ago tv, 'What's My Line?' A team had to find out someone's trade or profession by asking a strictly limited number of questions to which only Yes or No answers could be given. The way we played it, we had to invent occupations, because our real ones would be known; except that Treazy didn't know what Trevor did (well, neither did I), so she took on the challenge of asking all the questions herself.

A bit flirtatiously in my view (she kept calling him 'Mr Sandpaper' because of the rough stubble on his bald head), she had narrowed down Trevor's job to something not quite selling things in shops but at any rate to do with money and accounts. She had four questions left.

'Are you in a bank?'

'No.' Three questions.

'But you said you deal with cash all the time, Mr Sandpaper.' This was allowed as a 'recap' question. So there were three to go.

'Not cash but money,' Treazy mused. 'Are you manufacturing banknotes in a mint?'

'No. Banknotes are cash,' said Trevor.

'Fuck!' Treazy exclaimed. Jane raised her eyebrows.

'Two questions,' Trevor said.

'Money every day,' Treazy said slowly. 'But not handling cash. You're an accountant.'

'That's why I wear one of those dark suits. No – but nearly.'

'One question,' Jane insisted. She wanted to finish the game; with Treazy losing.

'I know – I know –' Treazy was saying eagerly, nevertheless pausing to get it right. 'You are one of those people – this isn't the question – one of those people my Dad says come and tell you what's wrong with a business that's not doing so good, and charges you so much you go bust *faster!*'

For the first time I saw Ridyard embarrassed.

'You're a con – a money con – a *financial* consultant.'

'Are you making that the question?'

'Yes!'

'Well, I am.'

So Trevor of the wilful bald head, the motiveless boorishness, the shabby, smelly clothes, belonged to a dapper profession with best management practices and the jargon of reassurance at its fingertips. And when I met him in the pub or the street he had come from a computer in an oak-panelled room where worried local businessmen went to consult him. Or he would put on best jeans and anorak and go to them, and observe accounting procedures and send in vast bills. I could not believe it. Nor could Treazy.

'Mr Sandpaper, you're telling a porky.'

'True or false then?'

'False,' she said.

'True,' Trevor said. Straight-faced and serious.

'You are joking.' I couldn't help saying that.

'No joke, Mike. No joke.'

The use of my first name was ominous. I was looking him in the eye with accidental curiosity, and it didn't do to look Trevor Ridyard in the eye. He looked back, very bright little eyes, very straight gaze, a basilisk. 'Anything wrong with financial consultants?' he asked with a broad, threatening leer the girls took for humour. So they laughed. Treazy reached across and slapped him on his knee, he grabbed her wrist when she tried to do it a second time, and she overbalanced and fell across his lap.

'That's enough, Treazy,' Jane said quietly. Trevor grinned at her.

What was it that made Ridyard attractive to them? I felt sure that shaving my own head wouldn't produce the same results. I once formulated a theory, deriving from my father's overheard maxim about sex and timing, that if you caught a woman on a day when she had briefly despaired of attracting better things than you, you had a chance. But why should this apply to two teenagers with someone three times their age? Even in the depths of Christmas?

'I'm surprised,' I said, unconsciously provoking Trevor.

'Get used to the world,' he suggested.

'Time for supper,' said Jane in the silence.

Treazy helped her with dishes of sandwiches and arrays of cheese, and celery in a glass vase. We ate, and didn't return to that topic.

As I coped with the food it came to me that I had absolutely been missing what was under my nose: if he did not repel Zilla and Treazy, Trevor could be attractive to Jane. There had been a dozen signs and clues, and because I couldn't think he was attractive to anyone I had unconsciously suppressed the suspicion. That was why he was here as the odd man out in the party.

But so was I an odd man out. Two spare odd men, then....

After supper I made the excuse of collecting up crockery so as to join Jane in the kitchen. Setting down a pile of plates, I had shaped my lips to say, in the style of our ancient confidences and confessions, 'There's something between you and Trevor, isn't there?' when she went past me, quietly closed the door and said, 'Bill's put them all in this *huge* scrapbook he's hidden out in the shed.'

I must have looked bewildered, because she added immediately, 'The photos. And he's put labels on the back and given them *marks*.'

'Marks?'

'Like for essays. A+, B?+, C-?-.'

'But does he know these women?' For a second, Jane was

interrupted by laughter back in the lounge.

'Christ, I hope not. You don't think they're grades for *performance*, or something?'

She began to giggle, but she was caught by a cough bringing tears to her eyes, and the tears were suddenly the tears of weeping, and who made the first move I can't remember, but Jane for a second time recently was in my arms, completely the same trusting, distressed, yielding, desirable woman as before.

'Dear thing,' I said softly, using my old, old phrase to her. 'You're not to think *anything* like that of Bill. There'll be an explanation.'

In my voice I could hear the insufficient consolations of the past, the spurious understanding offered to draw someone closer, the tones of the emotional trickster. Jane heard them too, broke away, swatted me with her tea-towel.

'You're a dear old fraud,' she said.

※

An old fraud. In that bleak pocket of days between Christmas and the New Year I began to feel my shabby, lonely conspicuousness very acutely. Smiles from shop assistants seemed to have a quality of mockery, patronising, pitying smiles. I could see that my clothes (that raincoat!) looked old and uncared-for. Unless an older man can be spry and smart he will look a paltry thing, grubby and disreputable. And it's much worse if you are given, or driven, to walking round by yourself. You can be picked out and shunned as an eccentric, a tramp no one cares to know, a dodgy non-dog-owner. You can be mentioned to social services or become familiar to the police. I resolved to brighten up my image. And yet a general despondency cramped all action.

One small, and one larger occurrence depressed me on New Year's Eve. I went for a walk and found the air uncannily clammy and mild. The sea was placid, not just no white crests on the waves, but no waves, hardly a ripple. I walked along the water's edge under

75

a sky of unrelieved and motionless cloud. I could not detect a tide coming in or going out. It was a lake of mercury. I looked among the dunes in case Rachel sat hidden away. She was not there, nor was she in any of the shelters or the Horizon Café. The small thing that lowered my spirits was seeing, on my way back, a sticker in a parked car: 'IF IT AIN'T GOT THAT SWING, IT AIN'T NO PLAYGROUND, MAN.' That seemed to sum up my existence as 1st January hourly came nearer.

The more deeply disconcerting thing that happened was this: On a radio jazz show in the early evening the presenter was playing 'special New Year requests from friends far off in space or time.' And he read out what he could not know was a postcard from the dead. 'After that dip into deep, deep blue with the wonderful Billie Holliday,' he was saying, 'let's switch to a feisty mood. Geoff Stedman, from Fieldenhurst, writes to suggest we play something for, as he puts it, his "fellow-sufferer at that God-stricken Polytechnic" – Mike Barron.' So here it is, Mike. "Honeysuckle Rose", in this version arranged, gift-packed and delivered to your very ears by –' But I failed to hear the name of the quartet. Or listen to the tune. I found myself wandering round this dismal house in the severest dejection, self-hatred and guilt. Geoff had probably sent in his postcard well before he left the Polytechnic, as a surprise, and it had only just come through. He was reaching out to me from the grave, telling me that –

I certainly didn't go to Jane's hotel New Year celebrations, as Bill and Rory were due to, though I was invited. I dreaded a more dangerous version of Christmas afternoon, the possibility of a drunk and combative Trevor Ridyard turning up. What I did was see the New Year in while I sat and re-read Rachel's many pages of autobiography, which she had copied out purely for me.

They began at the beginning.

Rachel was born in 197– [it read like that; the date was left incomplete] *into a family which was not going to understand her, there were not any early signs of this because*

76

she was a happy and a contented child at her infant school.

Her earliest memory is of seeing her small sister in a cot when she was herself only three, although she thinks she remembers grazing her knee on the crazy paving outside the french windows in the house they lived in when she was 2 ¹/₂ unless that was an incident her mother told her about later. Her creative writing talent showed as soon as she first went to infant school because she could spell and write already. In the afternoon of her third day she wrote a little description of her teacher's pet goldfish which was called Ludbrooke. She was taken along at once to the Head Teacher's room by her class teacher Mrs Wolfenden, and she thought she had done something wrong, all she remembers of Mr Hurd's reaction was that he was amazed and asked her if she had copied it down from something else.

There followed several further pages of school memories, escapades with friends, birthday parties, etc; nothing about her writing ambitions until –

By the time Rachel was eleven and in secondary school she was filling small notebooks with descriptions of the world around her, what happened in school and so on, and giving them away to friends as presents. At fourteen she began writing proper novels, but it was at that time she realised her parents were never going to understand her.

I noticed that so far Flamingo had not been mentioned, which was puzzling. She would be two or three years older than Rachel and a presence in her home during her childhood. The parents, of course, featured vividly.

Rachel's father let her mother run the family and the house completely, and busied himself with his work and his hobbies which included hunting for treasure in the surrounding area

77

with metal-detectors. Rachel at fourteen felt more grown-up than any of these people and took more and more to a solitary life of writing and thinking.

So in my meetings with Rachel in lonely spots two solitary lives had fortuitously converged...

I skipped, second time round, long passages concerned with Rachel's teenage years because I wanted to read carefully for signs and hints about the present in the final pages.

In the summer of 198- Rachel sat her A Levels. When her results did not gain her the place she really wanted she went through two months of terrible crisis and doubt, she knew now her future was creative. Her father had never found any treasure. Rachel lived for her own imagination and said that was the real treasure, and her parents thought this was madness, writing poems, and literally they believed she was insane.

So she lived like a penniless nomad wandering from spot to spot around her little home town which at least was by the sea, which she loved, it gave her inspiration. If she went to the quietest places she was not really in danger of meeting odd people, or being pestered or threatened, but her father became very inquisitive about where she was, particularly if she walked into the country away from beaches and crowds. Sometimes she even agreed to go with him when he went treasure- hunting, but she preferred to walk off alone on those days and join him later.

Rachel seemed to have been coming at last to the moment when she and I first exchanged names, almost three months ago. Realising it was that long ago appalled me. The unnoticed avalanche of days, weeks, months had covered a quarter of my year of trial.

Rachel liked walking along the Roman road in the area, Dibdin Street, named after an 18th century footpad, which was really a long muddy track which travelled from here most of the way to London. She remembered one day she was taking a walk there in the early part of the autumn, on from where her father had dropped her in the car.

This passage had taken Rachel to the foot of a page near the middle of her third and last writing pad. You can imagine I had been intensely eager to read on. But when I lifted the leaf I saw that this was where the narrative had ended. Since all the pages were in neat, uncorrected handwriting as if fair-copied from rough drafts, perhaps Rachel had already drafted an account of our meeting on Dibdin Street? And would give that to me in due course? Only with that would I really be able to gauge what she thought of her life *now*, and what she intended to do with it.

And what she thought of me.

*

When he knocked on the door of my room in the Polytechnic Geoff Stedman, would administer three slow thick thuds as at the beginning of French classic drama performances. Myself, at Stedman's door I always gave the tattoo of Fate beginning Beethoven's Fifth, three rapid lighter knocks and one heavier.

On hearing that, Geoff would shout 'Enter!' intoning the word as Hamlet's father's Ghost under the stone floor at Elsinore might call out 'Swear!' But on one particular January day, as cold and rainy as the day now on which I remembered this, Stedman simply said, 'Come in.' Perhaps he hadn't properly heard my knock? Rain, in a day-long unending downpour, was pounding noisily on the windows of the corridor behind me.

When I entered I saw the reason for Stedman's abandonment of custom. Dave Underhill, the two earrings fixed together in his right ear, sat nervously upright on the edge of one of Geoff's comfortable armchairs. Geoff himself, unusually, sat with his back to the window, behind his desk, in a formal attitude. For him to set the desk between himself and his departmental head was a bad sign.

I hesitated, nearly retreated again. Underhill took advantage of my arrival. 'No, come in please, Mike,' he said. 'We've finished, I think, haven't we Geoff?'

'I don't know, Dave,' Stedman said. Dave always used first names. Geoff rarely did, and to do so to his Head of Department was striking. Underhill muttered something about going as far as they could for the moment, picked up his filofax, smiled faintly at me, and left.

'What have you finished?' I asked Stedman when the door had closed. He rose from his desk, stretched, and was about to emerge from behind it when something happening outside stopped him.

His window overlooked the Games Field.

'Christ, look at that!' he exclaimed. 'Dennis Frostick may have been right.'

Through the unbroken slantings of rain bouncing off pools on the concrete walkways and the car park in the foreground, we looked over to the Field beyond, where we had stopped to talk to Frostick on the way back from the pub in the autumn. The patch of very wet grass was now a lake. Standing there today we would have been shin-deep in water. We thought we could see it still spreading out. A gust of wind created ripples, waves almost.

'It's tidal,' I said.

'Let's hope for no break in the weather. Underhill's easing me out at the end of the year.'

'He's *what*?'

My incredulity was to console Geoff, not an expression of any surprise. This had been coming. I had heard about Underhill's excuses: 'constraints', 'restructuring', 'modernising management procedures', 'performance indicators' etc. He had deeply regretted the need to declare three-quarters of a post in the Humanities section of the faculty of Human, Educational, Linguistic, Social and Contemporary Studies surplus to requirements. He had offered Stedman one-and-three-quarter days a week next academic year, and Geoff had utterly refused.

80

Underhill said he had fought hard with Reginald Torridge, Deputy Director in overall charge of staffing (and supremo of the Ballroom Dancing Society), for that concession. In reality, like Torridge (whose suspicion of Geoff had been encouraged by Dave) Underhill was determined to get rid of Geoff altogether, and it was a relief that he was declining to stay on for even a fraction of his previous teaching.

It was around this time, I believe, that Stedman began to go a little off the rails in his behaviour, and not just his pronouncements on people, literature, music, the arts generally; and politics, of course. He started to enact his own principle that going crazy should be diverting for your friends, not a bore and a burden. He had always been a traveller, but mostly just in the vacations. He now fell into a habit of taking sudden term-time week-end trips to unusual foreign places.

There was no reason for returning from one such trip to attend Underhill's Humanities planning meeting on the Monday of our notional mid-term break in February. He had nothing to do until teaching resumed on the Wednesday, and he was, in truth, being fired in the summer. Thus he didn't attend. But Geoff's method of giving uncalled-for apologies for non-attendance was novel.

He must have timed his intervention carefully, for the moment about twenty minutes after the start when Dave Underhill would be getting into his stride. We were all there, sitting on his post-modern, hard-on-the-arse plastic seats, balancing on our knees indecipherable print-outs from Dave's computer distributed the previous week, when the telephone rang.

Dave cursed, picked it up, listened, said 'Hullo?' several times and put it down again. A minute later it rang once more. The Polytechnic switchboard had a call from abroad for Mr Underhill. There was some negotiation with a foreign operator, presumably on a bad line because Dave kept asking, 'Can you please speak louder!'

Finally Stedman came through. Calling from Lithuania. Immediately he was cut off. In five minutes the process was repeated, on an even worse line. Geoff apparently said he would try for a better one, and rang off. When nothing happened for fifteen minutes we assumed he had given up. Then the phone rang yet again.

This line was beautifully clear. We could all hear Geoff sounding off vigorously at the other end, making from a hotel room in Kaunas his own contribution to the planning of a syllabus he was not going to teach. We could even hear the print-outs rustling when Underhill put the phone down to refer to his own papers. With a patience that thinly covered a seething fury.

My own phone at home rang at 11.40 the next night. Stedman was back in England finally, after various flight problems, and at the airport. Leaving in haste five days earlier he had parked illegally at the terminal. It was a time of bomb scares, and his vehicle had been investigated by the police and towed away to some remote car pound closed at that hour. Geoff had returned with no cash, and no credit card on his person (they were still unusable in Lithuania) to obtain any from a hole in the wall. Would I pay for his taxi if he called at my flat on the way home?

He had drunk well during his delayed return journey. I felt concerned about him. I said it would be easier and cheaper if I went down to fetch him, provided he could wait for the hour-and-a-half it would take me to get there.

Stedman was in a manic as well as an intoxicated state when I found him in the hall outside Arrivals. I asked about the phone calls to Dave Underhill. 'I did it in the interests of HELSACS,' he said, his smile suggesting a determination to be awkward until the very last, though in a style he could represent as helpfulness.

On the motorway he was squirming inside his safety-belt in a vain effort to find in his pocket a light for his next cigarette.

'You have a match?' he asked. 'Does the car have a lighter?'

'It doesn't.'

We were several miles from a service area. I don't smoke myself, never have, don't understand the compulsion. Stedman was gazing at the traffic in the roaring winter darkness. 'I have never really believed in motorways,' he said,' except when I need a light so badly I…'

'Fucking motorways,' I suggested. But received no response.

Suddenly – 'Mike! Pull over, can you? To the hard shoulder?' It was after a vast speeding truck had overtaken us in the outer lane, illegally, clouding us in toxic fumes; you must feel like a mixture of Wagner and Genghis Khan in command of a monster like that. I was thoroughly perplexed and scared by Stedman's order, but did what he asked without question. We stopped. He unhitched his belt and opened the passenger door.

'What's the matter, Geoff?'

No answer. Did he need to relieve himself on the embankment? No, he got out, and walked round the front of the car to the edge of the carriageway. He turned his head towards the traffic and was picked out and flashed by the headlights of cars thundering by. When it was momentarily dark in my mirror I saw him, in my dipped headlights, step out into the nearside lane, then the middle. He seemed to be casting around as if looking for something he'd lost on the ground. The white stick of the unlit cigarette jerked up and down between his lips as if he was muttering curses, which he probably was.

I was immediately out of the car and running towards him, though not daring to shout and distract his attention. As he wandered across into the outer lane, cars appeared behind us, frenziedly flashing and hooting. One swerved. Speed intoxicates, and downsizes responsibility. None stopped, naturally. Not their business, a man seeking to kill himself while they were on much more important missions. They would read about it in the papers.

Stedman reached the central reservation and was picking his way along it, head down. He had just under two feet of gravelled verge in which to walk. I swear that one car brushed his overcoat as it sped past. It also shed from its passenger window a cigarette butt which hit the tarmac of the carriageway in a little shower of travelling sparks like an expiring firework.

Stedman stopped. Turned, looked up the motorway to his left, took a few hair-raising slow paces out. Bent down. Walking on the hard shoulder, I had caught him up, was level with him now. He crossed to the hard shoulder again. He lifted the glowing butt-end he had picked up, and lighted his cigarette.

✳

'The *morals* of the town?' Ken Trench paused severely, scissors closed, and fixed my eyes in his mirror with his own grave, censorious eyes while he considered the question. I had asked this while we were alone.

'If it's *got* morals,' I said. As a student of politics I don't mind eliciting prejudice. I dislike it, profoundly, but it can tell you something.

'More perversion here than Ancient Rome,' Ken replied. 'You can buy anything you want, soft or hard, in the Rock 'n Rendezvous. Or, come to that, in the Royal British Legion. Provided you know who to ask and *how* to ask. As for –' He contrived a dramatic pause and a special stare in the mirror, haloing my near-baldness with still hands – 'As for – the other – Chap came in here the other day, stranger of course, says "Do you know any girls in this town who do hand-reliefs?" I says, "I don't know any girls in this town who *don't*." "With the greatest due respect," he says, "that doesn't help me a lot. I want to find someone who does it for *payment*." Well, that's your choice, I thought. It's the problem with this country. Old Mother Thatcher did her best, but I can't see Major taking up the baton. Not his fault. People have got low horizons, they want quick answers. They're not prepared to make the effort.'

'Could you help that chap?'

'I said, "Look at the newsagents' postcard ads. Anything about the Girls' High School Manicure Project, try the phone number. I can't guarantee, but..."'

Rachel had said she would phone me when I had had time to read her autobiography. Yet all this time she had been silent, and that was worrying. It was now *February*, I couldn't believe it. Valentine's Day. My birthday. There had been a Valentine from Rosie. And a birthday card, separately. Jane marked the day with a plain postcard, sending good wishes 'from me and Bill', writing that they were hoping to see me soon (for Bill's consumption; I had often been seeing Jane alone.) She had pointfully underlined the date at the top. Dennis Frostick remembered, and sent a typically salacious greeting, a slightly Art Nouveau card of Norwegian origin but with an English caption: 'How the Princess enjoyed comforting the Old Troll!'

This cheered me. Nice to feel cheered and reasonably well on one's birthday. At my age the experience of uncomplicated physical well-being is rare enough, so you use it when it comes. When I left Ken's shop I decided on some exercise to clear my head, try to reassess my situation, and give myself an appetite for a late lunch. Would there be a chance of running into Rachel on Dibdin Street? Unlikely the same coincidence would occur twice, but the improving weather raised my hopes.

*

People are not meant to drive up Dibdin Street, but they do. They leave one of the intersecting highways or lanes and see how far the grassy track can be followed by car. When they can go no farther they sometimes even get out and walk. I was walking along a stretch approaching a little coppice, all my path so far just about negotiable by car; and sure enough, just off the track and into the trees was a vehicle, parked facing outwards. But not just any parked vehicle. This was Bill Bramston's proudly-owned new car of last summer, the Volvo estate. I recognised the registration number, the figure 2-3-4. Accordingly I expected to see Bill in it, or meet him walking farther on, using a day's leave to enjoy the weather.

But then I paused. I could not see anyone in the car, the reason being that every window in its long body – windscreen, door windows, rear window – was steamed up. On the inside.

My first thought was that Bill's new Volvo had been stolen for a joy ride and abandoned here. I put out a hand to try a door handle.

But I held back from that before I touched it because the car had begun to move and rock on its axles. There was activity in the car, with more than one person involved, Opening a door (assuming they were not all locked) would have intruded on it. Besides, car thieves might have been younger and stronger than me.

As the Volvo trembled, and nudged its springs with the invisible movements of whoever was inside it, I stood aside in embarrassment. As I edged away, hearing the slight but steady creaking filling the silence of the countryside, it occurred to me that Bill's photographic dreams might have been being fulfilled on this spot. Should I tell Jane about this?

I decided to walk on, and keep an eye on the car from the shelter of some bushes some hundred yards away up the track. If I managed to stay concealed by foliage, there was a chance that an occupant clearing steam off a window might not see me. To other persons my lurking might indeed have looked suspicious (no dog), but Dibdin Street was deserted at this weekday hour.

It was a long time before anything happened. I realised that Dr Koning was correct about my increasing long-sightedness when I distinctly saw somebody rub a tiny peep-hole in the steam in the windscreen on the driver's side. Then the engine was started up. Only when the car moved forward was a wider hole made, by an invisible hand, as if the presence of an intruder had been sensed and the occupants wanted to be cautious.

The vehicle bumped forward over the grass, turned right, drove away hastily and hazardously towards the road, probably scraping its silencer on the ridge of grass left in the centre of the track above the ruts left by tractors. Then it had reached the near horizon in this undulating landscape, a tiny silver toy disappearing over it in the distance, sunlight flashing off its roof. I went on walking in the opposite direction for about an hour, but any chance of sorting out my own affairs had gone.

I had had fears about a battery warning light in my car, shining at intervals over the previous few days. As I drove back it was alight for ominously long stretches, but I ignored it and headed for the

Clifftop Continental. Although Greg had left the Old Soldier, it had become, through his association with it, a place I rather disliked. I had acquired a preference for the hotel bar, and as long as I didn't go there every day, or talk overmuch to Jane on any day, it was now all right with her for me to use it.

'There wasn't any time to get you a proper card,' she said when she passed through and spotted me in my usual window seat. 'But Many Happys, anyway!'

'You *could* have sent me a Valentine,' I suggested. She smiled, but the smile faded quickly, and I was sorry to have reproached her.

I had come here partly with the intention of mentioning the car, but my instincts warned me to come at it indirectly and start with some other topic.

I chose one I had not raised with Jane before this.

'Does Zilla still see that Treazy?'

'Oh, don't give me "that Treazy"!' she almost shouted. But she seemed glad to have something to be angry about.

'I thought she was rather agreeable,' I said. 'Very well-mannered – and mature for her age.'

'Mature! Exactly. She had a hundred and twenty pounds out of Trevor's wallet in five seconds while she was alone in the hallway. We couldn't prove it, but who else? Luckily I didn't have that amount in my handbag, only about thirty, but she had that. She had the small change from Bill's jeans.'

'Wasn't he wearing them?'

'Oh Treazy had her methods. She even had the foreign coins out of a pot Bill keeps in the bedroom cupboard. I lost a bank card I had to cancel.'

'Did you guess she'd be like that?'

'We should've, but we didn't. We knew she was being "difficult" at home but that was understood as part of the deal. We were too innocent. They're all at it. Zilla brought some stuff home from the New Year's party she went to at Treazy's parents'. I took it off her and flushed it down the loo. She's going to get it from us if she ever sees her out of school again.'

'Are you saying it was drugs?'

'*Of course I am*! We think that's what she was nicking the money for. Treazy was very *very* mixed up.'

'She seemed so intelligent.'

'I'll say,' Jane laughed scornfully. 'She was a little nympho too, *you* of all people could see that, couldn't you?'

There was a pause in the conversation. Jane didn't seem at ease.

'I've got to get on,' she said.

'Has Bill got the day off?'

'No. Why?'

'I thought I saw the car somewhere at lunch time.' I didn't say where.

'It had to be in for a service.' A quick answer, prepared and unconvincing.

✳

I sent for a mail order mackintosh. Consumerama was advertising a 'Spring Sale', but I tried a smaller store first and came out with a dark blue suit which proved bluer in the light than I had expected, and a magenta jacket I definitely liked, together with a paisley handkerchief for the breast pocket. That left just a pair or two of suitable Sale trousers to purchase if I could find them at Consumerama.

Dennis Frostick at the Polytechnic had once proposed a theory that you could become HIV positive by trying on trousers in a menswear department. Something to do with the vigour employed by the person trying them on just before you. I honestly doubted that, but thought about Dennis when I took a few pairs to a cubicle, first making absolutely sure that Greg was nowhere to be seen on this floor or anywhere in the store.

With three new pairs to try I took off my existing pair, so worn and dirty by contrast, and draped them over a chair already holding my overcoat, scarf, gloves, hat and jacket, the only hook in the cubicle having been broken. My left leg was already into the left leg of the first prospective trousers as I propped myself against the partition, when I heard footsteps running in my direction outside the curtain. Whoever it was dragged the curtains of the adjacent cubicles apart and cursed to find them empty.

Then my own curtain was opened. And Rachel entered, pulling it across again behind her.

'Mike, I saw you come in. I won't be able to stand it!' she gasped. In distress near to hysteria.

'Rachel! – stand what?' All I could think of saying to calm her. Rachel clung to me, the first physical contact she had ever sought. The trousers dropped to the floor around my left ankle.

'Stand working here!' As if I ought to know she was, and what else could she mean?

'I didn't know. How long have you been here –?'

'Nine o'clock this morning. My sister got me the job. You know my sister?'

'Flamingo?' I had seen her distantly downstairs as I came in. Rachel took no notice of the wrong name I had involuntarily given.

'My father was on at me to get a job and Vicki asked them.'

'They wouldn't allow you in here with a man customer,' I said. I was enthralled, but also scared of blatantly adding to my reputation.

'I don't care. We can talk here.'

'We can't!'

'Did you read my book?'

'Yes. Look – I've got to dress.'

Rachel let go of my arm and sat down heavily. My clothes were pulled off the back of my chair and clustered around her. My hat fell into a corner. I feared for my glasses.

'We'll have to talk somewhere else. I'll need my trousers.' She let me pull them out from underneath her. 'I was trying these on.' The new ones.

'Try them on. I don't mind.' She looked much less self-possessed and more agitated than I had ever seen her before. Paler.

'I was very depressed over Christmas and the New Year.'

'Were you at home? I haven't seen you anywhere around the town. I thought you might have –'

'I was away. But I'm a lot better now. It's just that I won't be able to stand *this* place. The *people*.'

Outside a voice called 'Katie?' It was probably the same Assistant Manageress who had had to cope with Greg's behaviour when he attacked me. I knew that if she found me in a cubicle with Rachel – with 'Katie'? – I would have far more of the blame for the incident attached to me. Fortunately the footsteps receded.

'You've got to go,' I whispered, as desperate not to be discovered as I was to keep her back. 'When is your lunch hour?'

'It *is* my lunch hour.'

'Would you like to go somewhere and talk? The Horizon?'

'No. The pub.'

'No.'

'The Swish Fish?' Rachel said.

'There won't be time.' Quite apart from the expense, I instinctively thought... But then I reconsidered. A proper talk with Rachel would be something different. A pity that one needed at least two hours when taking a meal at the Swish Fish.

'There'll be plenty of time,' she said. 'I'm not coming back here.'

'What do you mean?'

'I'm resigning now.'

This was a chilly winter weekday lunchtime, but the Swish Fish was nevertheless open. Empty, expansively warm, comfortable. We took our places at a table in one of the soft leathery alcoves into which the dining area was divided, ushered by an overwhelmingly suave and attentive waiter.

'Can we have some wine? ' Rachel asked, even before he could suggest as much as an aperitif.

'Of course.'

When he offered me the wine list Rachel grabbed at it, choosing randomly and rapidly, it seemed, but it *was* a Chablis. The waiter received the order with a slightly ironic smile in my direction, or did

90

I imagine that? The Swish Fish, with its impeccable decor and its candles lighted by manicured hands made its superiority very plain. There was nowhere else like it within twenty miles along the coast in either direction.

'We shouldn't have come here. It will look as if I've seduced you away from your work,' I heard myself say.

'You haven't. I resigned on the way out of the store. Sorry I never phoned, I was going to, but...' She smiled, pale and fraught but with brighter eyes. 'I wanted to ask you... But no, it doesn't matter.'

'Ask me what?'

'Some more about your house.'

'About my house. Why?'

Surprisingly for a cold, out-of-season weekday two more persons had entered, walked past us partially out of sight behind a centre floral display, and sat down. The style of the seating made it difficult to see them properly. They were across the aisle from us but farther down the room, and I had only the narrowest view of the man's back. I could see the woman's face but did not recognise her. The strange thing was that I believed I had seen the man somewhere else, though I couldn't place him.

'I'm interested,' Rachel was saying. 'Do you have the house to yourself? You don't share it with anyone?'

'No, I don't.' Why was she asking me all this? Unless –

'I want to find a room to live,' she said. 'I'd buy my own food and pay for the heating. I'd try to pay some rent.'

There are powerful moments in life when nearby physical detail suddenly becomes luminous. It took only as long as one, or two, seconds for that to happen to me now, for me to be aware of the views through the sea-facing plateglass windows, the forecourt between the restaurant and a low concrete wall bounding the esplanade. Beyond this wall stood red metal posts for the seafront lamps. Between these lamps hung strung-out wires regularly dotted with unlit fairy lights. Seagulls went about and about, swooping under or rising over the wires, soundlessly, like flying ornaments, hovering with feet tucked in straight under their tail feathers. The sky, uniformly grey over its entire expanse, was turning visibly greyer and bluer as I looked at it. Rachel was drinking the Chablis as if it was lemonade.

'You say you've got these rooms at the top, a whole flat. No one's going to think anything if I've got a flat in *your* house.' Why not? Didn't I have a reputation for something? I hoped Rachel wouldn't have heard about it. 'I mean, it's a big house for one person, you said. I asked the people where I've been if they thought it would be a good thing to live somewhere else, and they said, if I was still in the area and in contact with my family, it might be.'

From somewhere in the depths of the walls or above the pictures (and this seemed wrong for the Swish Fish, a black mark in the food guides?) muzak had started up, distant yet mesmerising: a slow, donkey-jogging tune in a minor key, subdued and doleful. The man in the couple sitting farther down seemed to be confidently propounding something to the woman in a voice that yes, I did recognise, but I could not place it. The woman was nodding and nodding, like a toy animal with a flexible neck.

'Where *have* you been?' I asked Rachel.

'I didn't tell you that, did I. I took a rest after Christmas. One that my doctor persuaded me to take. In a sort of hospital. I thought I could write there, but I couldn't. And it made no difference. Except, I realised I've got to live somewhere else. Though I knew that without going into hospital.'

I didn't go on asking where exactly she had been. I felt I was seeing for the first time something that had been 'under my nose', that I had been too insensitive to appreciate. I was confronted with a situation much more complicated than I had foreseen, and why hadn't I realised that from the beautiful Rachel's lonely and risky behaviour?

Along the esplanade they have, at intervals, telescopes in solid metal cases which swivel round on their stands to point in any direction. A 20p coin opens the lens for you for about three minutes, then the shutter falls and what was clear becomes dark again. From where I sat with Rachel in Captain Pedro's the two dark eyes of a telescope machine stared at me darkly over the esplanade wall. The situation had been suddenly clear to me, but whatever I did about it now, refusing or agreeing, would bring down obscurity. Two opaque lenses.

I felt watched by the dark telescope eyes. I felt accused. This was no good. I had to decide once and for all. It wasn't as difficult as I thought, because there really was only one reasonable course of action open to me when I balanced the practicalities of my relationship with Rachel against all my other circumstances. So I made my judgement of the matter completely clear to Rachel at once.

'I *cannot* provide a decent flat for you in my house. I'm sorry, but it's an *appalling* house. I'd be ashamed to let anyone else live in it (Rosie, though?) You can come and visit me there to see it, if you like. You never have, so I'm inviting you now, this afternoon. But not to live there.'

She looked disappointed, and fell silent as she ate.

I was becoming certain I knew the strange man talking to the strange woman in charming, practised tones. About I knew not what, because I couldn't hear what they were saying.

I said to Rachel, to break the silence, 'Look, I feel really bad about disappointing you. Will you come and look at the place? I think you won't *want* to live there when you've seen it.'

'O.K.' (That pleased me, of course...)

'Let's just enjoy our lunch now, and talk about something else. I don't have your manuscript with me, but we can look at it when we go back.'

'O.K.' (This was good...)

Now the man turned his head and lifted it, and called to the waiter, and I saw his profile. It was Sid Burgess who was making a smoothly assured, eye-catching gesture to obtain service.

Rachel moved into the house the following week-end.

✳

The afternoon before Rachel came it was cruelly cold, even for March. I'd been asleep in my armchair, one of those deep and awful daytime sleeps from which you wake not knowing who you are, where you are, what time it is, and wondering whether you have had a temporary journey into death itself. Again I had been dreaming about the Polytechnic, and unlike most dreams this one didn't fade as I resumed contact with real time and place. It had involved two actual events from around this time of year, one related to me by Geoff Stedman and the other an episode in which I had been personally involved.

The last rational, sane move that Stedman made in an effort to save his position at the Polytechnic seemed, on the face of it, quite well-calculated. He tried an informal, personal approach to Tim Hulzer, the Director. Geoff got on with Hulzer, who was known to be a jazz fan, and, for a chemical engineer, quite an aficionado of the arts.

And yet the entire attempt went crazily wrong. Hulzer was, after all, the responsible boss of a big concern. Geoff did not reckon on his being unwilling, on grounds of protocol, or just unable on account of time, to practise much relaxed goodwill. As Geoff was going to see him concerning his imminent sacking from the faculty, procedure required Hulzer to inform Torridge, his staffing Deputy, and naturally, Dave Underhill. They insisted on being present during what Stedman had hoped would be a friendly one-to-one chat. Thus Geoff was confronted and outnumbered by enemies, in a meeting which the union had not approved, another unhelpful factor. Before the encounter, however, Geoff had also managed to do something to alienate his only possible sympathiser, the Director himself.

He entered the outer office where Dilly Davis, Hulzer's secretary, was sitting. She smiled at him and said, 'Oh yes, Dr Hulzer's expecting you. He won't be back for five or ten minutes, but he says you can go in and wait for him if you like.' This Geoff took to be a good sign. Hulzer was being decent. He stepped into the penthouse office, for the first time ever, onto its thick carpeting. He took in a gleaming empty desk and shining leather armchairs, a thin eight-foot rubber plant rising out of a smallish wooden tub of black, wet earth next to a long sofa at an acute angle to the window; and especially he noticed a picture on the wall behind this sofa.

He wanted badly, while there was time, to take a closer look at this picture. From six feet away it appeared to be a small, very early Francis Bacon, an artist not long dead at this moment in time; if so, it was an amazingly prescient purchase on the part of the Polytechnic (or even Hulzer if it was a personal possession?) many years before, since it could not have been afforded at early 1990s prices. But one of the heavy armchairs positioned next to the sofa blocked off access there to the floor area in front of the picture, and so did the rubber plant at the window end, these obstructions being surely intentional.

All the same, with several minutes to wait, Stedman decided he would contrive a closer look. Sofa and chair looked too cumbersome to shift, so he squeezed past the tall rubber-plant (it swayed dangerously) and stepped up to the modestly-framed canvas, which hung by a thin chain from a simple hook screwed into the wall. In front of the painting he found himself utterly unsure whether it was indeed an early Bacon or the work of an imitator. Perhaps there would be a label on the back?

He told me that as he lifted up the picture from the wall and half turned it over he was conscious of a very distant ringing sound, more like a ringing in the ears than the clamour of an alarm bell. He gave it no attention. There was no label on the back of the canvas, no clue of any sort as to the identity of the artist. Carefully he let the painting rest again back on the wall exactly as he had found it.

As soon as he had done that he heard voices in the outer office. As he stepped hastily out of the enclosed floor space he brushed vigorously against the rubber-plant. It tilted sideways and would have fallen, but Geoff lunged forward and caught it by its trunk. Too energetically, because he uprooted it. All he could do was set it on its side on the Director's carpet. As he did so, Hulzer, Torridge and Underhill entered together.

'I'm afraid I've had a contretemps with your plant,' Stedman apologised.

Hulzer was prepared to show tolerance on that matter. 'An accident waiting to happen,' he said. 'No please, don't worry, we'll clear it up later.' But the meeting was off on the wrong foot. The arrival of three people to interview him instead of one person allowing him a confidential dialogue threw him completely, and Geoff thought he made his case much too weakly.

It was not to say that the Director's chairmanship was not scrupulously fair. Some of his questions to Torridge were pretty sharp, and he cross-examined Underhill (who had come without earrings) in a remarkably sceptical tone. But towards the end of their thirty-minute session, he made it implicitly clear that he would be leaving the final decision in the hands of Dr Torridge, who would consider the case in the light of the various factors they had discussed and let Stedman know the outcome. Geoff believed he might be offered a compromise, and told himself he might consider that on its merits. He thanked them all, politely, and apologised again about the rubber-plant, and they all stood up to leave.

At this point heavy footsteps were heard in the outer office, the door was thrown open without a knock, and three helmeted police ran into the room. Their eyes went first to the uprooted plant and the scatter of soil on the carpet. The sergeant at least must quickly have realised from the dress and demeanour of the three persons in the room and the protests of Dilly Davis the secretary that they were not burglars. But still he shouted, as if the habit were ingrained and the reaction automatic, 'Stay just where you are, don't move – any of you.' And when Dr Hulzer did move forward to explain, 'You got ears, mate?'

Of course the painting had been wired to an alarm elsewhere in the building, and also to one in the police station. Eventually the police took off their helmets and apologised, the sergeant proving slavishly polite and obsequious to the Director, who thanked them for responding to what could have been an emergency and offering to send Dilly Davis for coffee; which the police declined.

Not long after this, when Stedman had received Torridge's 'regrets that he could not advise Mr Underhill to alter his faculty staffing arrangements for the forthcoming academic year', came the disconcerting performance Stedman contrived during a dinner practice.

In their second year on our Catering Management course pairs of students were attached, strictly by arrangement with the kitchen staff's union, to the Staff Dining Room, where they gained experience of the ordering of supplies, the cooking and presentation of meals, the serving and clearing up, the keeping of accounts, health and safety regulations. Work started early in the morning but students stayed for the week of their attachment in a special small flat along the corridor; it was easier to simulate the work pressures of a hotel or conference centre if you were living 'on site.'

They had to imagine that on one evening, or even two, they were providing a dinner for important business visitors in the dining room of their apartment. And who would be better, as imaginary important clients, than their own lecturers, people they needed to please and impress? Parties of up to four 'corporate clients', male or female, sat down to dinner served by the students, who would usually join them for coffee as an informal conclusion to the proceedings.

A flu epidemic had hit large numbers of staff, which was presumably why the students had to scrape the barrel for people to role-play as business persons and came up with the unlikely male trio of Frostick (whose wife Anita cried off with the virus), Geoff Stedman, and myself. This time the host students were two young women, Sophie and Charley (short for Charlotte).

Stedman had been muttering mysteriously over pints in the pub that if the dinner required role-playing and simulation he would obligingly provide it. But Frostick and I were not let in on any plans he might have had. When the three of us met in the downstairs lobby at seven Geoff was carrying a sizeable suitcase. 'Back me up, the two of you,' he said. 'In what, Geoff?' we asked. 'You'll see.'

The students, wearing the nearest clothes they could afford that resembled those favoured by senior catering staff at the Grosvenor or Selsdon Park, greeted us formally but warmly. Stedman apologised for bringing the heavy suitcase, refusing help with it, dropping it clumsily into a corner of the dining room.

Stedman took a whisky from Sophie, declined water or ice, and sat down on an upright chair. He shifted the drink from hand to hand and was uneasily silent. Frostick and I played the game and conducted highly artificial conversation. Then suddenly, within the hearing of Sophie and Charley, Geoff declared, 'I'm not going to be very good as a corporate personage to-night.'

Dennis and I looked at him apprehensively. Sophie stood still, erect and trim, in unobtrusive attendance near the kitchen door, listening. Charley joined her. Neither of these two were taught by Stedman, thus had much less knowledge of how he might behave. He now looked deeply down into the last droplet in his glass and drank it off. 'I've been made homeless,' he said. I looked at Dennis and he looked back nervously. To challenge Geoff at once would certainly have been letting him down. But if the students believed him, how long could it be allowed to go on? When would it be letting him down *not* to rescue him from his own excesses? The young women's eyes were already fixed on him with some embarrassment. It was a good performance. And why should a lecturer in their Polytechnic be lying?

I recalled Stedman telling me once that he considered another of his purposes in teaching here in the miserable 1990s, apart from conveying the greatness of great literature, was 'to reactivate the spayed consciences of these young people.' But in to-night's display there was a lot of Stedman's own insecurity and resentment, and another touch of the madness he pledged himself to make entertaining to his friends if he ever succumbed to it.

'What's happening to your furniture?' Sophie now asked from across the room, forsaking all pretence of being the invisible manager.

'All in store already.'

'It hasn't gone to your new house?' Charley, with a concerned look.

'I don't have a new house.'

'But – your wife?' Sophie, smiling slightly.

'My wife – is leaving me.'

'Oh, I'm so sorry,' Charley said, believing him, and as if comforting someone recently bereaved. I just could not have imagined Stedman would go so far in his act. I really couldn't. Did he know something?

'That's all right,' he responded to Charley's condolence. The two girls had edged closer, had temporarily forgotten dinner. 'Sit down, please,' Geoff said. 'Just for a moment. There are various things I'd like to speak about. It won't take long.'

'Geoff,' Frostick put in, launching a smile to get him out of his selfsprung trap. But the intervention was cut short. Charley's concern rode over it.

'But where are you going to live, Mr Stedman? Where are you going *tonight*?'

'That's it. I have nowhere at all to go. I'd like to stay here.'

There was the completest silence. During none of this perform-ance had Geoff been smoking, a remarkable feat of abstinence. But now he asked permission to do that. He lit up with fingers he deliberately caused to shake, while the students produced an ashtray from somewhere.

'I don't think things are as bad as this,' I said. Dennis Frostick grunted in agreement.

'They're every bit as bad,' Stedman interrupted, angrily and abruptly. 'I've little or nothing in the bank to rent accommodation with, let alone buy. But – as I've tried to say – I'm not complaining. You can find people in a far worse plight than me any night in the City Centre. Haven't you seen them?'

Sophie and Charley perfunctorily acknowledged that. Frostick agreed and we tried to divert the conversation. We had our doubts about Kinnock but we'd be voting Labour next time. Stedman stubbed out his cigarette half way down, lit another with hands still trembling. He began to talk about homelessness in the city and the students brought the starter and a bottle of wine to the table. We were almost forgetting that Geoff was still referring to himself in his assumed role when – 'Have you ever been out late enough in the Centre to see that one all-night bus that circles the estates?' he demanded. 'One fare for any journey, of whatever length? You get people on that who've been begging all day for their food, and their fare for that bus. It's become a night refuge for the young homeless, travelling round and round. If it comes to it, I'll be on that myself tonight.'

This now had to be stopped as quickly as possible, before Stedman became so engrossed in his pretences that he could not terminate them of his own accord.

'Geoff!' Dennis stood up and confronted him. 'I think we should talk about this quietly for a minute or two somewhere else.'

But Stedman rose too, and side-stepped him, and went to the window to gaze out over the city darkness.

'But I shan't have to catch that bus because I know that people with consciences will help someone without a home to go to, and let me spend just this one night here. Until I get my bearings in the new life I have to face.' Sophie looked at Charley questioningly, but Charley looked just blankly bewildered. 'Perhaps by tomorrow night I shall have found just one loyal and understanding friend –' So wasn't I in that category? Or Frostick, who was just sitting slumped in cynical despair at Stedman's act – 'who will be prepared to help me. But to-night I've suffered the uncertainty and fear of thousands out there who have nowhere to go, not just one night but every night, as far on into the future as they can see. That is a feeling I implore you to appreciate.'

This behaviour (I have to say it of my friend and colleague) was a disgrace; but Sophie's face showed a degree of suspicion, a relieved smile was starting on her lips, Stedman's rhetoric having gone just a bit too far. Geoff noticed it, I think, and turned to Charley, who was not smiling, not prepared to doubt his sincerity.

'I need something out of that case,' he said to her. 'I... I just don't feel strong enough at the moment to lift it.' He sat down suddenly and exhaustedly on a hard chair. 'Do you think you could bring it over to me?'

Still tricked and anxious, Charley sprang up obligingly and ran to the corner prepared to lift something heavy. She bent over, put two hands to its handle, heaved. It proved as light as air. She set it down, bewildered, at Stedman's feet while Sophie laughed. Stedman opened it. It was empty except for a crumpled book of used air tickets. Charley was red with embarrassment and anger at being caught out. She told people about this. It did Stedman no good at all in the Polytechnic, though there was little that goodwill could now have done to save him.

*

I needed to have yet another tooth looked at. But that persistent glowing of the red warning light on my dashboard had brought trouble. The car wouldn't start at all on the day I had to go to the city and see Faulkner, so it was a case of a bus to the nearest railhead and a stopping train for the rest of the journey. And this was the day before Rachel turned up at the house with her belongings brought with her in their father's car by Flamingo, or, if you like, her sister Victoria. I could have done without the day in town.

Faulkner was not loquacious (he is never that) but he was in moralising mood. He settled my anxieties with a small filling undertaken in silence, then began a brisk cleaning of the rest of my teeth, telling me, 'You are holding up well, considering.'

'Considering what?'

'Your age. I suppose some time I shall have to face it too.'

This had to be humour, since I took Faulkner to be several years my senior, probably on the brink of the customary retirement age. But he continued without anything in his voice or expression to suggest that, as if he saw someone on his couch obviously older than himself. That depressed me.

'Our mouths are microcosms of ourselves, 'he continued. And I wondered what was not: what about our hands, our feet, our anything? 'We live and die by what we ingest, and our teeth are the instruments by which we conduct that process. Our pleasure and our suffering – and our self-respect – are to be found in our teeth.' Faulkner was a National Health dentist, but the sudden purple passage reminded me of the cant in the glossy brochures of some private practitioners. 'You are a drinker of alcohol, I take it? Wines and spirits?' (As if that required explaining.)

'Yes – I suppose I am.'

'Only rarely of sweet fizzy drinks?'

'Scarcely ever.'

'Good! Stick to the alcohol, especially the spirits. Less of it passing over the teeth – I assume. And whisky doesn't hurt them anyway.'

The extra time required to return to the coast by train and bus meant that, despite Faulkner's encouragement, I didn't bother with the usual post-dental drink (certainly not in the Firkin Beaver) after rising from the couch, but hurried off through the beginnings of a small spring snowstorm towards the station.

Perhaps the station bar, though? No. My train would be in soon. I just walked up the platform watching snow settle on the lines.

The InterCity train to London was due in a few minutes before mine, and was already announced. It would come in on this sharply curving platform and, at this time of day, pick up no more than a dozen or twenty people. I strolled slowly along thinking of Rachel arriving in twenty-four hours, and took in the newsstand, the buffet, the Ladies' and the Gentlemen's. At that point I turned back and went into the Gentlemen's, and stood at an urinal no larger than a porcelain ashtray. Over it someone had written on the wall, 'Thank you for not wanking'. In my mood of anticipation about Rachel I would have appreciated that more if someone else had not added, 'Oh, I thought I was.'

I walked out again and on up the platform past empty sequences of luggage trolleys, past windows set in nineteenth century grey brick walls, of lighted offices where computers flickered on desks at which young men in shirtsleeves worked in aggressive central heating. There were green benches at intervals along the platform. On the last bench of all, just before the point where the roof ended and the snow was falling in the open air, sat a figure, a girl with a green rucksack on the seat beside her; I thought she would be about sixteen or seventeen. Her yellow T-shirt said SCUMBAG STREET, and below it she wore a black leather mini-skirt allowing an effortless crossing of longish legs in white tights. But what most of all drew my gaze was hair streaked in a mixture of pinks and crimsons and rising from her head in a kind of tatty, congealed fountain.

'Hullo,' she said. I answered with only a nod. If I thought I recognised her it was only because I had seen several girls like this on the streets of the city and may have stored the memory of this hair at the back of my mind. I had almost passed her when –

'Can I ask you something? How fast will the next train be going when it reaches *here*?'

An alarming question; the more alarming for being asked in a calm, assured way as if just wanting interesting, harmless general information. About the speed of the incoming InterCity.

'It will have slowed up, 'I said.

'It won't be going fast?'

'Not *so* fast.'

I walked on, out into the snow for a few paces. When I turned, she had left the seat and was carrying the rucksack in the direction of the far end, where the London InterCity would be arriving quite fast, any minute now. I began to follow her quickly, as she paced determinedly along the white edge of the platform.

I came up beside the exit to the station hall – ticket windows, timetables, shops – and in front of me a man with a foreign appearance dropped a much-labelled suitcase on the ground and felt in his pocket. As I reached him, he found his ticket, looked at it, cursed.

'Please,' he said to me. 'I think I have the wrong ticket for making my travel to London at this time of day. You wait here with my luggage while I go ask?'

'Certainly.' Instant, instinctive helpfulness.

But what about the girl? And if there were explosives in that suitcase, timed to go off when the InterCity appeared? I looked round for a station official. There was none. I saw the girl stop and drop her rucksack, and stand still on the edge of the platform at the farthest end, away from any other people, out from under the roof at that point, snow falling on her. At that place, or so I imagined, the driver of the London train would only just have seriously applied his brakes.

I realised at last that I did know her. It was Treazy, Zilla Bramston's friend of Christmas afternoon, who had left the Bramstons' home taking every item of paper money and small change she could lay her hands on. Treazy with different hair. I was certain she had not known who I was.

The owner of the suitcase had not come back. The labels on his property hinted at danger in an almost crazily comprehensive style; could he really have taken in Beirut, Belfast, Baghdad, Bogota? For my own safety I had to leave it. For everyone's safety I had to find a station official. That also for Treazy's sake, Treazy who, in the distance, was looking up the line, her rucksack left lying on the platform behind her.

I would not be easily forgiven if I abandoned property trusted to my care and it was stolen. But as the tannoy announced the imminent arrival of the London train I did just that, to rescue Treazy first.

But as soon as this decision was made, I saw the policeman appear from nowhere and speak to her, and lead her away by the arm from the platform edge picking up her rucksack with his free hand. And then the owner of the suitcase was back at my elbow, innocent and fulsome in gratitude. When it came in he swung his burden, with all its ominous labellings, safely onto the London train.

✳

What would it mean, Rachel (or Katie) coming to live in this house?

In those few days I had cleared up obsessively in the dreadful upstairs flat. I left the lounge and bedroom gas fires on for most of the time to take off the lethal chill and damp that had invaded it. I invested in brand-new linen for the best of the beds, I transferred the least objectionable crockery and cutlery from my kitchen to hers. I tried to look at every room in the entire house with the eyes of a young woman in her late teens, although I didn't really know how this particular person would see things: I didn't really *know* Rachel, did I!

'You've met my sister Vicki,' Rachel said at three that Saturday afternoon. 'At the theatre that night?' The snow had settled, but had stopped falling. The light made the two tall thickly-wrapped blonde girls with pale faces even more intriguingly attractive. Out in the road I could see the old Austin Metro which Vicki/Flamingo had driven here, stacked up unbelievably high with cases and boxes. This was moving in with a vengeance.

'Yes, and before that I met you at...'

I was unsure about how to refer to the previous encounters, but Flamingo interrupted my hesitations.

'You say there's some kind of different way into the house, or something?

'Well, yes, 'I admitted. I had rather hoped Rachel wouldn't require the separate access to the flat. 'There's – let me show you – there's these rather steep steps.' We walked round the side and I indicated them. 'But why not come up through the house? It's warmer.'

'No, this is fine,' Flamingo/Vicki insisted. 'You have a key?'

I picked it up from the hallstand and she almost snatched it. I put on an overcoat. We trudged up the icy iron stairs and she unlocked the door opening onto the kitchen. She did a fast tour of inspection of all the rooms and came back smiling.

'It's fine. And what you said to Katie about rent is still on?'

'Yes, of course.' A fiver to be paid at the end of each week to cover heat and light, and nothing else. No agreement, no rent book, no formality. This payment I only really asked for so as to ensure regular reasons for seeing Rachel/Katie, just in case she chose to lead as lonely a life here as anywhere else.

'I'll help you with the unloading,' I said.

'No we'll do it ourselves. You go in the warm,' Katie/Rachel said flatly.

'Honestly, it wouldn't be a problem for me.'

'No!' 'We insist you *don't*. Really.' The two of them spoke together, an emphatic refusal to let me have anything to do with it. 'We'll knock on the door when we've finished.' They both smiled, a puzzling moment of amused embarrassment.

'Won't you have some coffee first?'

'It's all right.' Vicki insisted. 'We've settled everything, haven't we?'

'Well yes, but...'

I retired reluctantly, feeling obscurely outwitted. As they began to unload I wanted to pry, though I did not wish to be seen prying. If I stood behind the lace curtains in my bedroom I could see a slice of the hatchback door of the Metro, with Rachel and Flamingo lifting goods out of it. But they worked fast and I couldn't clearly tell exactly what they were taking in; apart from what seemed to be some fairly large black boxes, glimpsed for less than a second before they were carried upstairs very fast. It was odd to hear footsteps, albeit muffled by the layer of snow, going up and down the iron staircase seven or eight times. I was to become used to the sound in the following weeks.

Eventually the unloading stopped. I saw the hatchback door had been closed. Their voices upstairs were discussing something, though I couldn't hear what was being said; and there was laughter. Then there were footsteps on the outside stairs again and a knock at the front door.

'That inside door to the flat – have you got the key for that?' Flamingo it was, standing there and briskly asking me this. What could I say but Yes, and hand it over? To say, She wouldn't need that, would render me suspected of wanting to enter the flat when Rachel was not there; or even when she was. Flamingo proceeded to enquire about my own movements and the hours I kept – 'So that she won't disturb you.' I told her about my regular shopping habits and pub visiting hours and bedtimes.

106

'She's not to get in late,' Flamingo required. So what role and responsibility was she expecting of me when the two keys gave Rachel such freedom and independence? 'And you can tell me if you're not satisfied in any way. Can you think of anything else?'

'Only that you are both very welcome to come in and see me any time you like.'

'Oh well, yes, I know. Thanks... Right then!' And she went out to the Metro and drove away at once, scarcely pausing to say more than 'Bye. Thanks.' She drawled the words as if she was not speaking to someone who had done her sister and their family a kindness by opening my premises for Rachel's virtually free use; one could see it that way. I could have made some conditions about my personal right of access to my rented accommodation, asked some reciprocal duties of Rachel. But I didn't. Vicki's uncommunicative briskness prevented me thinking all this through there and then, on my feet. The element of businesslike determination in these two young women was something I hadn't bargained for...

I was sitting in the lounge wondering when I could safely creep upstairs and listen for the sound of Rachel in the flat – still an enchanting idea with some potential in it – when I heard the upstairs outer door slam suddenly. Rachel clattered down the steps and walked off rapidly down the street in the direction of the town centre.

✳

She left, and returned to, the flat very frequently, with no clear pattern in times of departure and return. Mostly she would half run, confidently, down the steps and be gone before I could reach a window to see which way she was going. While she was out I gave much thought to devising plausible excuses for contacting her, but produced none that would not seem transparently suspect. When I knew her to be in, I took to listening to see what I could fathom from her movements upstairs. There was nothing I might not have guessed.

Oh yes, I listened under her bedroom, heard shoes falling on the floor, imagined the room and the new linen, could just hear the bed creak as she stepped into it. And what did that tell me except that she undressed and slept and got up again?

At the end of the first week an envelope containing a five pound note lay on the mat. I dared to write a note of thanks and wondered if Rachel would like to drop down for coffee some time? At the end of the second week the envelope brought five one pound coins and thanks for inviting her but she was busy, and I might be interested to know that she was finding the flat a good place to go on with her writing.

What if I pretended one night that I had left my front door key in another coat, and I was knocking at her door so as to gain access to my part of the house via her inside door? No, that seemed artificial and obvious. I would have just to listen and wait for any chance that fate convincingly provided.

One evening in that second week I caught sight of Rachel going out with Flamingo in the Metro. They had descended the staircase slowly together once, then gone back for something and come down a second time carrying boxes. Was this a moonlight flit? No. They came back, late, again negotiating the staircase twice, sat talking up there with animated voices for half-an-hour. Then finally Flamingo left in the car and Rachel went to bed.

In that second week I also heard heavy male feet on the stairs one afternoon and imagined the father coming to visit; although it seemed a heavier and more vigorous tread than I would have expected. The next day, in the early evening, the same feet went up and I heard the door slam and their owner come down again. He was not visible from my window. Whoever it was did not arrive in a car.

The Clifftop Continental had become my evening as well as my occasional lunch-time resort. But one night I found the boisterous business talk at the bar too much to take and gave up on it after a couple of halves. Back at the house by nine I noticed as usual the light shining in Rachel's quarters. It was windy, and I could hear no sound coming from there until I turned the key and pushed open my own front door.

I thought I would be admitting myself to an expected silence in the house. But it was not silent. Not in the least. It vibrated and echoed to a curious whirring and rattling, a quick staccato thundering, a noise nothing to do with the faulty fridge, or the water-pipes, or the wind browbeating the walls. Rachel must have found a jam session on the radio, something Flamingo would enjoy, perhaps they were listening up there together? But it went on continuously, without introductions or intervals. So it must be jazz on a cassette player, with a strong percussion element. Tapes of Flamingo's?

I liked jazz, while lacking Geoff Stedman's profound passion for it. I liked jazz drumming. But I didn't feel prepared to listen to it against my will and so intensively. An hour went by. Another hour, or so it felt. It was eleven. Eleven fifteen. The music, the drumming, was not going to stop.

So this would be my excuse for making contact with Rachel. I would be friendly, naturally. I would knock and enquire the name of the combo she was listening to. I would ask her, and Flamingo too, if they were there together, if she would like some coffee, even a drink. Anything to stop it. I would not stand in the cold at the top of the iron stairs, but go to the inside door and knock loudly enough to be heard and answered.

When I did that – several heavy slow knocks – the drumming certainly stopped for a moment. But oddly the rest of the music went on. I heard Rachel calling out, 'It's not locked.' Interesting. I opened the door and went in, and along the short hallway to the lounge. Now the drumming resumed.

In the lounge Flamingo was seated, with long, stockinged legs elegantly extended, behind her entire array of percussion instruments. It was the way she had sat in performance at the Constant Hope and she was dressed as she would be with her Quartet. But she was absolutely alone. It had been her calling out to me to enter. I realised at once that this equipment was what she had been bringing in in mysterious boxes with Rachel's belongings, that the cassette-player on the sideboard had been providing jazz without percussion, and that Flamingo had been providing it. She was a good drummer, fast, inventive. But not so good doing this without my consent above my head.

So one sister had persuaded me into giving her virtually rent-free lodgings and the other was using the house for drum practice... All this under my nose, and I had not expected, or realised...

'You don't mind?' she asked quietly and gently, not drawling, just naturally and nicely. And smiled very warmly and vividly, rearranging her hair a little.

'No... I don't mind at all.' I heard my voice changing my mind for me.

'Our Dad doesn't like me practising at home. And if I'm practising here, it's easier for me to keep everything here and call for it when I've got gigs.' She put down the two brushes with blood-red bristles with which she had been stroking a drum when I entered, and rose to switch off the cassette player. 'You told me the nights you usually went out. She doesn't like to stay in while I'm practising, either. Oh, that reminds me. She keeps meaning to give you this and forgetting. You might as well take it now.'

It was a brown A4 manila envelope, sealed, and filled with something.

'Why didn't she want to give it to me herself?'

Flamingo smiled and shrugged.

'I've hardly seen Rachel – Katie – since she moved in, 'I said. She was looking at me and nodding. 'Can I make you some coffee? Or would you like a drink?'

'Coffee.'

She followed me downstairs. We sat in two of the cavernous and battered armchairs, one on each side of the electric fire with the faintly flickering artificial coals. Her eyes roamed around the room.

'Who is that?' she enquired about the Christmas photograph of Rosie. Beside which her Valentine was still standing. 'Is it your wife?'

'I've never been married. It's a friend. She sends me cards.'

Flamingo went over and picked it up.

'Her Christmas card with a photo is *still* on the sideboard at the end of March. She's a real friend. It's her writing on the Valentine, yes?'

I thought this rather attractive audacity, but audacity for certain. I didn't want to be questioned about Rosie and changed the subject.

'How is your job going?'

'My job in the post office? Well that *is* going.'

'How do you mean?'

'It's privatised, isn't it.' She made a cynical, ironic face. I was about to say that the Post Office was one of the few things not yet privatised, but then she went on rapidly. 'Or franchised, or something. It depends on Consumerama to keep going. If Consumerama goes, so will the post office.'

'Consumerama won't go.'

'Didn't you know? Consumerama's going down the pan. It's closing in the summer. I'll be down the job centre unless someone else takes me as a package with the franchise.'

This upset me, as does any unforeseen change of any kind. Something solid and expected — Flamingo cool and elegant behind the glass screen at the back of the store — was actually to vanish?

'But I'm tired of slogging on at a counter. I'd rather concentrate on music. I'm working on it.'

'I realised that,' I nearly said. But instead I asked, 'Are you getting gigs?'

For a second she adopted the defensive drawl again, but then, as if remembering not to use it, reverted to the friendly, relaxed voice.

'Oh. yeah, yeah — everywhere,' she began by saying. And then, 'One last week, and one... One next month.' She mentioned two pubs farther along the coast, but unenthusiastically. Then — 'There was something about a *local* place starting up music and entertainments in a bar. Old-fashioned stuff mainly, but... Do you know anything about that?'

I had no news of anything of that kind.

'Mike, what I thought was — you like jazz, and you've only just moved here from the Polytechnic —?' I agreed that yes, I had. 'Do

111

you know of any venues in the city we could try? You probably belonged to clubs and things, and knew all about that? Or jobs there? I'd like to get away from home.'

I was silent with surprise. I, who had been impressed by Flamingo's slim and spindly beauty in the post office and behind these drums (but I must get used to 'Vicki' before I called her Flamingo to her lovely face) now found that she was impressed by something about *me*. I was a sophisticate from the city and would know about jazz venues and job prospects in the city.

'You've done a lot of things for Katie,' she went on. 'Reading what she writes and everything. Can you do anything to help me and the others getting gigs?'

Had I done much for Katie? I played for time, not wanting to offer anything I could not provide.

'I think of her as "Rachel". That's what she...'

'Oh that "Rachel" thing, yes. My sister likes to have her other personality. She's been ill, you know. You realised?'

'She's told me a bit.'

'Katie's very mixed up. She had another spell of the depression over Christmas. She wouldn't join in or anything.'

'I can understand.'

'You know she's been like this on and off for five years?'

'For five years? But she took her A Levels last year and did well.'

'She took her A Levels five years ago last year. She was diagnosed just after she sat them. Katie's twenty-four – nearly two years older than me.'

'Katie's *older* than you?'

'Yes.'

All the innocence I had wanted to protect and exploit in Rachel was suddenly transferred to Flamingo.

'Flamingo,' I said, 'I can't believe that.' Vicki looked up at me very sharply and strangely. 'I'm sorry – I was thinking of somebody else... Look, I go to jazz, but I really don't know a great amount about venues, and I don't know anyone who sets up gigs.' She looked disappointed, so I went on, 'All I can say is that I would be willing to think about it and *try* to help.'

This was lame, but it restored Vicki's smile. She took a gulp of the coffee and looked at me meaningfully, without blinking, over the top of the cup. I stayed silent, looked at her. Looked.

'And you really don't mind that I've been practising here?'

'Not the tiniest bit.'

She continued to look. And lay back in the frayed depths of the chair, kicking off her shoes and yawning, and smiling because she had yawned.

She had stretched out her legs in the course of the yawn, patting the air three inches above the carpet with her toes. Now she put her feet down to rest on the carpet only just in front of my own feet and said, 'Thank you, Mike.'

It was only her second use of my name to me, and it made me aware of the very first use a few minutes before. I got up and took two steps towards her as she lay stretched out. At that moment we both heard Rachel's footsteps pounding up the outside stairs. So I sat down again.

※

As March lengthened it grew callously colder, continuing the frost and occasional snow, typical of the ever-lurking malice of that month. But one Saturday morning I woke up sweating in bed to find, when I opened the curtains, that a rapid thaw had been going on. Everything was wet and flowing, the sun shone strongly, and the day would surely bring people out to the countryside and the sea. This produced the first of what I tend to regard as the three attempts on my life; though perhaps that is a slight exaggeration.

The afternoon was dry, lustrously sunny, very warm for the time of year. I decided to go for a long beach walk. I was alone, but the long stretches of sand are so vast that my twenty or so fellow-walkers were scattered very widely over the low-tide expanse. Some were among the dunes, some at the sea-edge, and every one or pair of them

113

appeared to be accompanied by a dog. Even at this distance I could hear, across the calm air, these animals being called or encouraged or instructed or chided. From far away they looked like insects crawling inquisitively over a flat surface of off-colour cheese.

The sea was not mill-pond still, but it stirred only a little, and under the unclouded blue of the sky it looked black and heavy, it glittered like metal. No lip or border of foam crested its ripples. Among seaweed and perennial driftwood the tide had left one light bulb which I picked up, wiped dry and pocketed. You never knew.

I had a good reason for a bracing walk: a letter from Rosie, the first for many weeks, which blatantly breached all of our agreed rules. It proposed a hypothesis: assuming we did make a life together from August onwards she really did require to know soon where we might live. Her flat, which she had continued to occupy, was not somewhere she wanted to stay. (It had too many associations?) But was my rented house suitable for a permanent arrangement? She might be prepared for us to live there temporarily if she joined me for the end of the summer, but we might need to make plans for somewhere else beyond that? All this just *assuming* we teamed up, of course.

But hypotheses were in danger of merging into *faits accomplis*. Rosie was pressing me to make a decision before I had any intention of making one. So when I replied it would be with a humorously formal reminder that all these matters depended on our joint decision, and mere practicalities of this kind should not be allowed to pre-empt it.

'Dear Rosie,' I said out loud. Then I realised that I was not orally composing a reply but affectionately addressing her across the many miles of land between us. That surprised me. Last October I might have caught myself saying 'Dear Rachel', and more recently 'Dear Flamingo.' But an undertow seemed to be pulling me back towards Rosie. What I had not achieved with Rachel or Flamingo, or even particularly tried to achieve where it might have been possible, with Jane, had yielded ground to the one scenario offering a real chance: Rosie's agreeing with any wish of mine to marry her.

I paced the level sand enjoying the sunshine, the mild air, the calm to which not even the sea provided much of an audible background. But wasn't there some curious extraneous buzz in the landscape? Was it the vibration of invisible traffic on a far road? I looked around me, gazed at the grey-blue and yellow distances of sea and beach, the sand ending miles away in front of me on a horizon. On that horizon I saw a dog.

And it was suddenly rising into the air above its apparent owners, two tiny sticks apparently waving at it with microscopic gestures. At first, distance reduced its height as it flew, it looked as if was only an inch or so above the beach. But as it buzzed nearer it was clearly airborne at a height of about a hundred feet, over the fields away to my right. And now, as it changed its mind and its direction, it was not a dog at all, or a flying insect, but something resembling a small canvas-winged motor-bike. It was out over the sands again, and flying towards me.

Less than a couple of hundred yards away it was making to fly directly over me. But then it was suddenly losing height, descending, swooping down, all this in seconds. It was roaring and spluttering down directly at me. Its noise as it dived was terrifying, ear-destroying. And its intention was surely to land not just in front of me or beyond me, but *on* me, hitting me, running me over. It was aimed at me, I was its target for smashing and mowing down as it landed.

I don't know when the pilot of this microlite realised that if he hit and destroyed me he might also kill or injure others. It must have needed an instantaneous decision to swerve a few feet and avoid the small family with the genuine dog that had just happened to come down out of the dunes and run out across the sand. At the time I believed this aviator only changed his mind because of them – or because of their dog, which was the creature he was most likely to hit. Had I been alone he could have mown me down and left me for the tide to carry away and deliver somewhere else along the coast, with injuries which the sea could easily have inflicted or concealed by its own action. But as things were, I thought, a dog saved me.

Firmly on the sand some twenty yards beyond me the man braked, and switched off the engine with a shaking, snorting splutter. Then he dismounted. He was a short thick figure, garbed in material somewhat like the wings of his deadly craft. Helmeted, goggled, gloved. One solid gloved hand went up to the goggles and lifted them onto the helmet. He covered the space between myself and the beached microlite with fast, aggressive steps. Reaching me he pushed his face into mine and –

'Knew it was *you!*' he said. 'Tell you a mile off.' He gave a leering, menacing smile, and I believe Trevor Ridyard would have tried another means of disposing of me there and then if the family with the dog had not been coming over.

'Should have had my machine-gun with me. Never mind. Another time.'

I suppose I smiled. The family dog now joined us and sniffed at Trevor's boots. I patted it. The father of the family, a young man in anorak and jeans and woolly hat with a pom-pom came over to fire questions at Trevor about his machine. He was flattered by this attention, and I won time. But I waited until they were both fully absorbed in technical exchanges before nodding a cursory goodbye and making my getaway back to where I had parked.

The incident had been preposterous. I had to know from Jane just what this man had against me and how I could avoid further murderous incidents like this. She would not be at the Clifftop Continental, this was a Saturday afternoon. I would have to risk calling in at their home. But Bill was likely to be there, and the children...

Then something happened to render my indecision irrelevant. A mile along the road back to town I overtook Jane herself riding the old blue bicycle, Bill's, still unsold, a man's machine but Jane was obviously finding it useful. I drew up ahead of her. She saw me, stopped, put a foot down on the ground, got off, rested the bike against a field gate.

'Bill has the car this afternoon,' was the first thing she said.

'Where have you been? I was on the beach and – '

'I had to see someone about something.'

'That's very mysterious. I've just seen Trevor Ridyard.'

'*When?*'

'Just now.'

'*Where?*'

When I reached the words 'a microlite' she looked horrified, was shaking with fright.

'You mean he went straight off and? – He was flying that thing just ten minutes ago? I've begged him not to until someone's seen to it… It's been going wrong. He *promised*.'

She seemed unable to contain her alarm and anger. A horde of bullocks was gathering at the gate where we stood, heads over the top wooden bar, vaguely hostile and breathing determinedly but still friendlier-looking than Trevor.

'Jane,' I challenged, 'Any time I've ever met Trevor he's been bloody awful to me. You and Bill know him much better than I ever will. What's it about?'

The bullocks lowed and grunted. Jane waved them away. They tossed their heads and stayed put, listening. Eventually…

'There's things to tell you about Trevor,' she began. 'Not now. When there's time. Bill…'

But she paused, not intending to disclose what Bill thought at this moment.

'Anything more to tell me about Bill?'

She grabbed at that very eagerly.

'Yes. I've found a video.'

She described it. I was astonished.

'I can't risk showing you at home,' she said. But had I asked to see this video at all? 'I'll have to bring it to the hotel one day. And show you there?'

✳

What if I replied to Rosie's letter with practicalities and she proposed abandoning our agreement and moving in at once? How would I deal with it if Rachel was still in residence when Rosie arrived?

One dark early evening I put my hand into the pocket of the new raincoat I had been wearing on that beach walk and found the light bulb I had picked up. I pushed it into the socket of the lounge table-lamp – and it lighted. Weakly, but it stayed alight. Some sort of lucky omen? I pulled the curtains and sat down for about the twentieth time to devise a response to Rosie's request. I heard Rachel go up the outside staircase hurriedly, and slam the door.

No peace. Only a few moments after that I heard the heavy male footsteps I had several times recognised, ascending the metal steps and stopping at the top. It could have been a rapping or knocking at Rachel's door that I heard next, but I wasn't sure. Then the feet came down again and walked away.

And ten minutes later Rachel was herself running down, without closing her outside door. I went out to the hall, intending to go up to my observation post behind the bedroom lace curtains. But something was falling on the mat: a note. As I picked it up I could hear Rachel hastily returning upstairs.

It said:

Dear Mike,
Please will you contact me as soon as possible.
Love,
Rachel
xxxx

Possibly she hadn't realised I was in. The light by which I had been studying Rosie's letter had not been strong enough to penetrate the thick curtains. It was easier, as I was at the front door, to go up the iron steps (so I suppose that was how I must have been spotted by someone still in the street.) To my first knock there was no answer, as if Rachel thought it was too soon for me to arrive. I

118

knocked louder. A crack of the door opened and she let me in.

'You've had my note already?' She looked pale and apprehensive as she closed the door at once behind me. 'That man's been coming here again.'

'What man?' Who on earth would Rachel expect me to know about? I only knew Bill, and Trevor. I'd heard footsteps I'd taken to be her father's, but 'that man' was a contemptuous phrase for even an estranged girl to use about her parent. 'That barman,' she added.

'Barman? Not...?'

'From the Old Soldier. Greg. He's after Vicki, you knew that? He's been warned. He daren't go to our parents' house so he arrives when he thinks Vicki might be coming *here*. He saw us in the shops and turned up in case we'd come back together.'

'That man is not coming anywhere near this house!' I shouted. 'Does he know *I* live here?' After the Old Soldier and the Consumerama menswear department, was even my own house to be a no-go area?

'He doesn't realise *who* lives here. I *think* he doesn't. He watches, though. Vicki's told him she's not going to be here and he's not to come, but he was here five minutes ago. It's after he knocks off work at his new job. He's done it three days running. When it's getting dark.'

'You don't – let him in? Has he ever been in?'

'No!'

'If I ever see him I'll call the police.'

'He's had the police onto him already. He's had a caution not to stalk. There's only one thing you *can* do.'

'What's that?'

'Forbid him yourself. You can see him where he's working. Or wait for him next time he arrives here'

'I'm *not* going to tangle with that man. The police will have to handle it.'

She sighed with heavy impatience. But there were no circumstances in which I would either confront Greg at his place of work or countenance his coming within ten miles of *these* premises. I was resolved on that.

There was a crash downstairs, at the front of the house, a loud single sound of glass shattering.

'Wait a minute. No...' I turned back from the outside door, 'Do you have the key to the inside door?' She produced it from the mantelpiece. 'Come down with me.' There were limits to my lonely courage.

This time I did need the key, the door being locked from the inside.

Together we stood on the first floor landing. Everywhere was dark, and for a second I feared that Greg might have obtained entry and be preparing to smash things. We waited until we were certain there was no movement anywhere in the house.

I entered the silent lounge, switched on the main light and found the table lamp on the floor, the bulb extinguished. The brick must have been impeded by the curtains, but penetrated the gap between them and hit the lamp, which lay on the carpet beside it. Very sharp edges had been left in the broken window by the impact. Some of the glass had fallen on the sofa, some between the sofa and the wall.

'The police will have to come *now*,' I said at once, and went to the telephone.

The young constable came after an hour when were finishing the first coffee Rachel had accepted from me in my house.

'Hullo, sir!' he said cheerily at the door. Was I supposed to recognise him...? He spoke as if we had obviously met before.

'Do I know you?' I asked.

'Oh I've seen you around, sir, I expect,' he replied cryptically. An intimation that I was a familiar figure in the town? I told him what had happened, who I thought might have been responsible. I had no surname for Greg, neither had Rachel. But he was identifiable from our descriptions.

'The problem is, sir, as you'll appreciate, that we can't be sure without witnesses to the action itself, that it *was* this particular individual involved. Any one of a half-a-dozen persons might have thought they had reasons for giving you trouble.' Oh might they?

120

Was I as notoriously unpopular as that? 'Well, in a manner of speaking there might. You're a face different people might know.' He snapped a rubber band round his notebook. 'If you can manage to get a sight of him next time, either of you, let us know and we'll be very glad to do what we can, sir.'

✳

When both the constabulary and Rachel had left, I boarded up the broken window with cardboard, took a drink, forgot Rosie's letter, and settled down to look again at the autobiography, because Rachel's last words had been about whether I had read it, and was I going to tell her what I thought of it, and talk about it with her? At one point at the kitchen table, while we had been drinking the coffee and waiting for the police, Rachel had sat nervously threading and unthreading her fingers, and I had placed a hand over both her hands and kept it there, caressing them reassuringly. Rachel did not respond at all to the gesture, removed one hand to pick up her cup and lifted the other to straighten her hair.

At that moment I felt that there was little mileage in this pursuit of Rachel. And also, if Greg was positively determined to revisit and even attack me, I would need to say something quickly about her writings, because the safest and most sensible measure I could now take – what if I had been sitting on the sofa when the brick had arrived? – was to require Rachel to move out. This would be a depressing end to what could have been a beautiful situation, but...

Rachel's account had continued from where the first instalment left off. But interestingly, not in the way I had imagined. She was always surprising.

Rachel had done a silly thing by leaving her writing notebook in the car down the slot next to the passenger seat because the book was new – when a book had writing in it she kept it in her hand all the time she was out, in case anyone

121

read it, and hid it when she was at home in case anyone
discovered it while she was out of the room.

But that was an accident that gave her the chance to think
about herself on the walk and she made two decisions in the
hour she was walking. One was that when she finished writing
the story of her life she would go back to poems, and the other
was that she would leave home.

So there were two persons meeting on Dibdin Street while
engaged in profound cogitation about themselves and their futures.

Rachel knew that life at home with her father, mother and
sister, even though her brother away at college meant there was
more peace and quiet, was impossible for her creative abilities.
Her sister had learnt drumming for the school orchestra, and
was very good, but she needed a quiet place to practise because
she was playing professionally now.

On that walk across the fields on that Roman track that
afternoon, she didn't see a rainbow like the girl at the end of
the D.H.Lawrence novel, but it came to her that there would
have to be a person, somebody, who would turn up out of the
blue and be the answer to her problems.

Was this the wisdom of hindsight? When I reached it I was
reading with fascinated eagerness. But I had to wait longer for any
revelations about myself, because Rachel now started on many
pages of digression about books she had read, and accounts in them
of characters meeting fateful people who had changed their lives.
Even when she came back to the day we had met in the country she
first of all took the story away in a different direction.

There was another reason why Rachel decided to walk
along the Roman road that day. She had begun to be a bit
afraid of going near the sea. When the weather was hot she
sometimes took her swimwear to the beach and bathed,

sometimes with her sister and sometimes alone. But that summer she stopped going alone because she had a rather scary experience. She was only a quite good swimmer, not a very good one, about six lengths of a swimming pool had been her limit at school. But one day in a fairly calm sea she found she just wanted to swim on and on and out and out.

She started to be afraid she would swim on and on until she actually knew she could never get back. The tides either going out or coming in along this coast are very treacherous.

Therefore she more often walked on Dibdin Street, when her father would take her there and soon had a conviction this would produce an accidental meeting with someone who could help her, because you sometimes met interesting strangers on this Roman road. But her sister went on going to a remote part of the beach for a private swim.

And that was the last page of this manuscript, which had come on handwritten pages rather than in a writing pad and which I had been reading in bed. So I shuffled Rachel's neatly-written sheets together and pushed them back into the A4 envelope in which they had been passed to me by Flamingo. Or tried to. Because I then realised I had left a few sheets inside the envelope by mistake when I had taken the others out. And they continued the tale.

Several times on the beach she had seen a tall elderly man with glasses and a gloomy look walking to and fro obviously interested in her but too timid and polite to speak. He didn't look peculiar or dangerous and she even said Hullo to him once because he looked lonely. Now this same elderly nearly-bald person was walking towards her on the Roman road, as if fate had arranged it! If they were meant to meet, she would definitely stop and speak.

His manner and his way of speaking put her off at first. He looked like he was trying to hold his face together with painful effort to stop it falling apart if he opened his mouth too wide.

123

Maybe it was shyness because he never did it later. Or maybe it was toothache. She felt sorry for him, and found out his name was Mike.

After this she had various meetings with Mike, in the café at the theatre, on the promenade, in a pub and a restaurant and he told her he had a large old house in the town. She went on walks up his street and thought that this house was somewhere she could live and write.

One afternoon she went to see the flat at the top of the house with Mike and she had to fend off attempts by him to chat her up and make passes at her. [That sentence was vigorously crossed out but I could make sense of it.] *But he did it so badly and was so easy to resist that she thought having her own keys to the doors of the flat and keeping out of his way would be enough protection, and the rent of £5 a week was an offer she could not refuse.*

This last paragraph was not intended for me to read. The story had broken off at the foot of a page and it was only when I happened to turn over that I saw, upside down, the last paragraph written at the top with a line through it and the one sentence ineffectually erased. Rachel had used the clean side without remembering the paragraph she had written and cancelled on the reverse.

It settled it, though. In a letter to Rachel I contrived a mixture of regret and firmness. I said I didn't want my house and my person put under threat from Greg's obsession and violence (just as much a threat to Rachel) and therefore could she please think hard about finding somewhere else to live? I didn't enjoy the thought of either of us living in danger or the house under police surveillance, and if there were more trouble I might be held to blame by her parents.

To Rosie I wrote a correct and businesslike letter but made it clear that *if* we were to live together when our year expired, she might make *provisional* plans for arriving on a specific date in August and preparing herself to stay in this house for the remainder of the summer. In that period we would discuss future accommodation plans. And yes (she had asked about this), she could in that event bring a few of her own chattels to make the interim life more comfortable. But I had still not committed myself, had I! I thought I made that transparently clear.

The outside door of the top flat has no letter box, and there was no way in which my letter to Rachel would go under the door. I had to push it under the inside door, and I suppose that is how she missed it. That is, if she did miss it, not ignore it for her own reasons. All I know is that my letter appeared to cross with one from her next day which enclosed a month's rent in advance, and said she had a chance of 'going away somewhere to do some writing during the coming weeks' and would see me later.

✳

Meanwhile, was one expected to call this spring? The wind was icy, and whined in the chimneys. The showers were not warm and rejuvenating but full of malicious sleet. There were power cuts due to cables having blown down. I had a particularly long and vindictive cold.

And then things softened. The wind fell. The flattened daffodils in the gardens recovered a more virile posture just as they were fading (analogy for my present life in a natural detail like that). The rain warmed up. If I had not been summarily 'retired' from the Polytechnic, I would, at this time of year, have been lugging home boxes of students' essay files and dissertations, as I had for so many past years. And giving them advisory grades in advance of their *viva voce* examinations.

The art was to praise and upgrade your own students as much as you dared, hoping that an overburdened external examiner would just rubber-stamp the Polytechnic verdict. The students were not supposed to know about the Polytechnic's own role in the grading process, but of course they knew everything.

I had several promising dissertations to appraise in my principal capacity, as a Politics lecturer. There was, for example, 'Ramsay Macdonald: the Quiet Revolutionary', a study of overlooked minor social legislation passed by the Labour Governments of 1924 and 1929-31. Or there was 'Elected by Elites,' an attempt to assess from Hansard whether the occupants of the old university seats in the House of Commons enhanced the intellectual content of debates. And best of these was 'The impact of the bicycle on Liberal electioneering in Wales, 1892-1905', which traced the usefulness of the new machine in assisting to power the fourth and last government led by Gladstone and the first and last led by Sir Henry Campbell-Bannerman.

But seventeen years ago, even then in my fifth year teaching at the Polytechnic, I already had a part in grading the more modest efforts of students presenting work for Auxiliary Modules. And one case in particular came to mind as I saw a warm April sunshine embrace at last the rooftops of the town.

'I – want – an "A",' Melanie repeated, for about the tenth time one afternoon. We were on the bed in my then flat, she had taken up a position kneeling threateningly over my prostrate body with my hands trapped on the pillow, and she was reiterating her demand by bouncing her bottom on my midriff.

I knew that Melanie's chances of an A grade in her Auxiliary Module were not considerable. In the written paper in June she might with luck achieve a B-. Not for knowledge or insight shown in her 'General Arts' answers, but for a concise and lively style supported by clear handwriting, always a help with tired examiners. In the viva, on the other hand, matters might be swayed by Melanie's very ample charm; much would depend on the susceptibilities of the examiner to whom she was allocated. Unfortunately the 8,000 word dissertation (on a General Arts topic chosen by the student with the tutor's guidance) might bring her down; there was no real chance of much more than a C+.

That afternoon – 'I want a *promise* of an "A" before we do anything else,' she blackmailed.

I had been through this process with students before, but none had tried as hard as Melanie.

'I *can't* promise. It's up to the Visiting Examiners.'

'Oh that's rubbish. You *tell* them what the grades are to be, everyone knows that.'

'Look – the Visiting Examiners have the final word. Ow!'

But then she gave up for a moment, sat back, retreated into a humorous yet ominous resentment.

'Do you mean to say I've yielded up my fanny to you for a miserable "B", or something? My fanny isn't worth an "A"?'

'I'll do what I can. I really will try. But I can't promise anything at all. It's in the examiners' hands.'

'Who's my particular examiner?'

'We don't know yet.'

'Tell him I've sacrificed the only fanny I'll ever have to the cause of your second adolescence, and I'll expect an "A" and nothing less.'

'It might be a "her".'

In the event it wasn't, and Melanie was very lucky in that respect.

The whole Department gathered in a meeting around a table in a seminar room in the Central Building, chaired by Dave Underhill's predecessor, the humourless and hawkish Clive Jepson. The specialist dissertations having been dealt with (a lengthy process) we ran more rapidly down the list of students of Auxiliary Modules. Each tutor read out his or her guidance comments and proposed grades, and we felt entitled to make points about our colleagues' assessments if we had taught students they had supervised.

Melanie's dissertation was on 'Food in the Fiction of the Forties', thus encompassing wartime and post-war shortages and rationing; her parents and grandparents would have had experience of all that. What subtle formulation, not too modest, nor too exaggerated, could I use to influence her Visiting Examiner?

This is a spirited, discerning student [I wrote] *whose work has matured encouragingly and shown a venturesome,*

127

original quality. Her performance in this Auxiliary Module matches her strength in her Main Options [Melanie's Catering Management grades were likely to be good] *and confirms a pleasing, even impressive, all-round ability. This is a well-documented and intuitively appreciative account of the treatment of food as a sub-text in the English novels of the era of Winston Churchill and Clement Attlee.*

Recommended B+/A-.

That was as far as I dared to go. But, given my ignorance of the literature of the period (if not the politics, which was why I was allocated the study to supervise), I felt moderately satisfied with my phrasing, and hoped the Visiting Examiner wouldn't be tempted even to lower that B+.

All this had to pass Jepson and the others first, so I dropped my voice on the A- as I read it out to the meeting. I saw Stedman's mouth drop open in incredulity. Stedman had strong views, and used strong language to express them, even then. He also believed in the strictest moral rectitude in judging students' work. I could see that he was shocked at my assessment of Melanie and would probably accuse me later of lacking principle. But he would not betray me in a meeting, rightly seeing me as an ally.

'*Discerning*? Melanie Robertson *discerning*?' Jepson commented. There he had fallen into my trap. After haggling over the word for a minute or two, I agreed to drop it, allowing him to score a point and pride himself on his vigilance. Time was short, and I believe he entirely overlooked my proposed grades; which the department secretary accordingly typed into the schedule for the examiners.

Of whom, that year, there were three. Dr Bridget Keegan was from the Sheerness Institute of Higher Education, Professor Collinson from Suffolk University, Mr Lapwin from what will soon be upgraded into the New University of Leatherhead. If Melanie had Dr Keegan, whose standards were almost sadistically rigorous, she was finished. Collinson was hard-nosed but reasonable, a decent man. Lapwin, on his first stint as an examiner, was an unknown quantity. Melanie fell to him.

He was a tall, gangling, neatly-suited, youngish man with a quick, nervous smile. He was full of enthusiasm (I listened to him with feigned fascination) for his work at Leatherhead, in his first academic post. He appeared eager to strike the students as fair. He looked a goodish prospect for Melanie, and I felt encouraged. During the morning break for coffee and éclairs (we always sought to treat the examiners well), I found out he was at work on a book about the supportive males behind famous feminists; not a bad sign for Melanie, who would be a feminist when it suited her but unquestionably warmed to men. She and the shy Lapwin might get on well in the viva situation.

He came happy out of his morning interviews with the students. He accepted the aperitifs and wine which Dr Keegan, next to him at table, declined, and enquired, 'Now who should I look out for this afternoon?'

I refilled his glass, and checked that Jepson, who was trying to impress Professor Collinson, was not listening. I was careful not to mention Melanie first, citing a few others casually before adding, 'But I'm forgetting one of the sharpest – Melanie Robertson.'

'Melanie Robertson,' he echoed. 'Yes. The dissertation was fine, I recall.' Only 'fine'? That was better than nothing, though. 'Yes, well... That's interesting.' But did a small cloud of doubt cross his forehead?

In the afternoon interview order I had managed to have Melanie placed after a somewhat silent mature woman student and before two very ordinary and colourless men. After these final four vivas came the tea break, and after tea followed our departmental session with the examiners. I hoped that by then Melanie's personality would remain more vivid in Lapwin's mind than her work.

The mature woman student underran her time, so that Melanie, who arrived with twenty minutes to spare, went in early. I lingered near the door, heard animated conversation. Then heard a laugh (Lapwin's), followed by louder laughter from both people in the room.

The next student arrived; he took a seat outside the door. Melanie had by now used her additional time, and was well into her own allocation – then was overrunning it. The conversation and laughter in the room showed no sign of stopping. I knocked, very discreetly, opened the door, smiled round it. Melanie and Lapwin were not sitting opposite each other in two easy chairs as provided, but side by side on a settee, with her work spread over their two laps.

'We won't be a minute, Mr Barron,' Lapwin said. And laughed.

They were several minutes; the viva ran to twice its scheduled length. As they emerged, having obviously enjoyed the encounter, Melanie said, 'Right then, I'll hold you to that.' It turned out to be the promise of the loan of a book he had told her about, in which she had expressed passionate interest.

Outside their door they stood and shook hands, warmly. Lapwin patted Melanie on the shoulder, and leaned towards her. For a moment I thought they might be going to kiss each other on the lips, or Lapwin would at least kiss her cheek. Then he drew back, smiled, and just said, 'Farewell, then, Melanie, good luck!' and let her go. But he watched her along the corridor and waved back when she turned to wave at him from the top of the stairs.

'That's quite a girl,' he said. I nodded. At that point Stedman came up the stairs, probably overheard Lapwin, looked hard at me, and passed on.

In the meeting, to Jepson's obvious frustration (had he cultivated Collinson too strenuously?) a favourite student of his was reduced by the professor to a B- from a B+. Most unwisely, he contested the judgement and Collinson dug his heels in, pointedly looking at his watch.

'Melanie Robertson,' we came to at last, and Jepson grinned very disagreeably in reading out the name. But Lapwin smiled eagerly.

'I think I can say better things of *this* student,' he said. 'In fact, I'd go farther than Mr Barron's rather muted comments. I found Melanie in every way a thoroughly intelligent and perceptive young woman.' So much for 'discerning', then. 'For a Catering Management student – which I believe she is? – she showed real adventurousness – about literature I mean – in her interview with me. Mr Barron hesitated between B+ and A-. I shall be raising that to a straight A.'

I saw Jepson cast on me, for a few astonished seconds, a look of profoundly hostile disbelief and envy. But he said nothing. He was not proposing to bargain a lower grade for a student in his department. But Stedman's look said more. His honesty was complete, his personal behaviour utterly scrupulous. I guessed that he silently deplored what had been going on between Melanie and myself. When he looked across at me after Lapwin's speech his expression simply said, 'You are a very fortunate fucker.'

Possibly Lapwin took away an enduring memory of his viva of Melanie, because she also came out with an A for the written paper she wrote in Finals three weeks later. I confess I let her think I had pulled remarkable strings to achieve the result she had demanded. But our connection went the way of so many teacher-student affairs not ending in permanent partnership; or even just ruining another relationship, or a marriage. A few months after leaving the Polytechnic Melanie was firmly wedded to someone else, Bill Bramston, and started using her second name, Jane, which Bill said he very much preferred. I 'kept up with them', as I have hinted (well, with Jane I did), and frequently wondered whether her home cooking didn't owe something to the resorts and devices of those 1940s novelists.

*

Where had all these months gone? Time had been prodigal with me in a most underhand fashion, devouring me like a cormorant on the local shores; it was past Easter now.

Had my mind been made up for me by my own indecision? Was my failure to put away Rosie's photograph a sign that I wanted her physically there as well? She was sending me ever more practical letters, trying, I thought, to pre-empt my choice of a future, acceding to my wish to stay in this house for the summer at least and talking about how her goods might help furnish it. I replied helpfully yet noncommittally, but caught myself tidying up even more parts of the house.

And where was Rachel? No letter came. Upstairs there was constant silence, no voices, no percussion practice, no heavy footsteps on the outside stairs. I tried speaking to Flamingo/Vicki in the post office, but much of the old distant elegance had returned. She told me first that she didn't know where Rachel was and when she might be back, then finally she let drop a hint that she had signed up for a term's course to help her writing and wouldn't be back until it was over. She declined the idea of meeting to discuss the whole question.

Perhaps Flamingo nudged Rachel to be in touch. Because, wonder of wonders, one day a postcard came, an artist's sketch of an unidentified house in an unnamed rural spot, and Rachel said she was very happy doing this (as if I didn't need to be told what 'this' was) and looked forward to seeing me soon. She signed it with her customary four kisses. This was the most elaborate communication I had ever had from Rachel, and I put it on a kitchen shelf. But I still didn't remove Rosie in her air hostess pose from the lounge mantelpiece.

I still forbade Rosie to phone me, so that when the phone rang it had to be either a sales call or Jane saying, 'Hi, it's me!'

'Hi, it's me! I'm in the hotel until four – with some time to spare. Are you free?' This was just after one o'clock.

'Yes, but why…?'

'I've got that video. Wait for me at the door of the bar.'

All I needed to do was to load up two black plastic bags with personal junk cleared from the house in case Rosie ever arrived: I intended to go on from the Clifftop Continental to the Recycling Complex. I drove off more eagerly than I could explain, and was in the hotel by 1.30.

In my recent visits I had noticed the preparations for a substantial refurbishment of various parts of the building. The place

132

could do with it, I thought. All of this was now in progress. The bar itself was boarded up.

'Upstairs!' Jane was suddenly whispering in my ear, as she came up to me standing outside the closed bar looking at the sunshine over the sea on this mild early May day.

'Who comes here out out of season?' I asked her, genuinely intrigued to know how it kept going.

'The adultery trade?' Jane suggested. 'That accounts for most accommodation income. Mrs Dunning and the directors think we'll be repaid for these alterations. We're the largest hotel for twenty miles. People hope they won't be noticed in a remote place if they're swallowed up in a large establishment. So they come here sooner than the little B&B's.'

We took a narrow back staircase up to the third floor, where a silent corridor began with frayed old carpeting and pot-plants on stands, then turned a corner past drapes and dust sheets into a smell of recent paint and a much more modern and luxurious atmosphere, a whole newly-revamped wing. In the air already was the faintest buzz of muzak, issuing from shiny new black speakers set high up along the walls. We stopped at the end door, which like all the others was as yet unnumbered, and Jane produced a key.

Inside was a fresh and clean, renovated bedroom which had evidently not been used yet.

'You've forgotten the video,' I said.

'I haven't. Wait.' She smiled.

She went over to a corner where a brand-new television set faced the kingsize double bed, on which I sat down among uncovered pillows and duvet, clean folded sheets, blankets. On top of the television was a card providing instructions for its use, including what you had to put into a slot if you wished to watch the in-house entertainment. Very up-to-date.

'I've put the video into the system downstairs,' Jane told me.

She switched on the set, fed it a couple of pound coins, and adjusted buttons and knobs to locate Bill's video, relayed to us from below. The screen shuffled parallel lines, snowed, buzzed unobligingly, then delivered without introduction a clear though unsteady picture of a woman. In a lavishly-equipped kitchen this blonde in a miniskirt with her rear to the camera was whisking something in a bowl.

When she turned and saw the camera was watching her, she did a badly-acted double-take, dropped the whisk, pulled down the skirt (it covered no under-garment) and flaunted herself naked around the kitchen, nude from the waist down. Then she picked up the whisk from the bowl – it trailed threads of creamy material – and perfunctorily patted her ample pudenda with it a few times. Some of the creamy stuff adhered to her vaginal hair, and she dipped into the bowl for more.

Then the camera focused on the kitchen door, through which arrived a brunette dressed in an aggressively smart, conservatively-tailored costume with a longer skirt. This one feigned, unconvincingly, a stern surprise at seeing the blonde and the illogical daubs of creamy strawberry whip on her loins. She knelt down to take a closer look at this phenomenon (while the blonde eagerly froze and let her do this), and the camera took a close look at a badge on the lapel of her costume: COASTAL COUNTIES BUSNESS GIRL OF THE 90's, spelt like that. With a forced smile its wearer began to lick the cream from the pudenda while their owner feigned an ecstatic approval.

Other displeasing sequences like this followed. They involved the peeling of bananas and a blending of honey with *crème de menthe* so that the 'BUSNESS GIRL' could present nipples smeared with the mixture for her collaboratrix to lick off. It was an amateurish effort, but unsettling for me all the same. To steady my hand I gripped Jane's where we lounged a bit uncomfortably on the bare double-bed mattress.

'Are you really thinking Bill shot this? I don't –'

'Bill's had a video camera for years, we've got films of the kids growing up.'

The girls on the screen, now both completely naked, had retired to a shower, where there was play with jets of warm water and faintly phallic bars of soap.

'But who *are* these people?'

'How do *I* know?'

'Does Bill know them?'

'Enough to video their fun and games, evidently.'

It was a bitter tone, but Jane's voice broke on the last word. I pulled her close to me in sympathy.

'Oh Mike, dear old Mike. There are other things to say when I feel I can. I wish we could go back.'

'We could go *on*, dear thing.'

The old pet name came so easily. But how oddly it came out of my much older face when I caught sight of it in the wall mirror in this room.

Jane's head was now on my shoulder. I stroked the slightly wiry, now greying hair that I had run my fingers through so often so long ago, and not nearly enough in the intervening years. So much of that enthralling past, evoked by remembering the crazy months of my involvement with 'Melanie', now seemed to be stirring inside me again. Could it really be that my year here was bringing me to this, not to Rachel, or Flamingo, or Rosie, but to the oldest remaining love I still had in my life? I knew I felt, sex apart, such a deep and innocent affection for Melanie/Jane. Such a need for her...

She pressed her right leg against mine, drew up her left knee, shifted onto her right side. On the screen the blonde, out of the shower, took a warm towel from a rail and began to rub down the brunette, giving special attention to her erogenous zones. Jane saw it, and lifted her left leg, and lay it across my thighs. I pushed up, against its soft pressure, and took her shoulders in my arms and kissed her. And repeated, and deepened, the kiss.

But we could hear voices outside in the corridor.

'Sod! I didn't fix the door,' Jane exclaimed.

Someone was trying a key, finding it locked the door instead of releasing the lock, pressing on the door handle, pushing at the door, entering. First the end of a suitcase came in, then the rest of it with a hand on its handle; and then, carrying it, dressed in a smart but very old tailored overcoat, a man, Sid Burgess.

135

'Ah! Do excuse me,' he pronounced clearly and politely, as Jane and I sat up, she with a curious little yelp of frustration.

'What room are you wanting, please?' she asked, with considerable self-possession in these circumstances. 'The even numbers are on the other side. This is 311.'

'I'm *so* sorry.'

Behind Sid Burgess we could hear a woman's voice in the corridor, asking perplexed and disagreeable questions. He ignored them and paused for a few seconds, almost a stage pause, giving Jane and myself a good stare, then switching his gaze to the activity still in progress on the screen. That look was a look of severe sorrow; as if to say, 'I gave up my life to clean family entertainment, and the world has settled for that.' Then he retreated.

'I know that man,' I said. 'I recognise him from the stage. He's called Sid Burgess.'

Jane jumped away from me in horror, landed her two feet on the floor beside the bed, then stood up and switched off the television in trembling agitation.

'Oh Christ, *no!*' she half screamed. 'You're not telling me that was *him?*'

'You've heard of him?'

'Yes. And I'm going to be working with him. He's signed a contract with Mrs Dunning to take over the new bar when it's finished.'

'He's *what?*'

'Sid and Beryl Burgess, yes? They're moving in. They're going to live here on a two-year contract, to start with. They'll be "theme hosts" in a Variety Bar.'

So Flamingo's rumour about a new venue for musical entertainment in a place in the town had been partly true. The new Variety Bar of the Clifftop Continental Hotel was to have a little dais at one end, with theatre curtains, and photographs of famous entertainers along the walls, and decorations reminiscent of 1940s variety venues, and Theme Nights of light entertainment booked and produced by Sid and Beryl. Stars of radio, television and film, they would end up as glorified barpersons in a seaside hotel.

'And the first time he meets me it has to be like that!' Jane went on, still aghast at the realisation. 'What sort of impression does he get of me?'

She straightened the bed (I helped) and ushered me out of the room, looking up and down the corridor first and listening hard. All we could hear was talk going on in another room, Sid and Beryl Burgess conversing in loud and clear tones, stage voices, they couldn't help it.

'Do you realise, you've never shown me any of the original photos?' I said. 'Will you?'

'I would, but…'

'But what?'

'He's hidden them in the album, somewhere else. If I *could* find them I'd chuck them over the cliff.'

We dropped our voices as we descended the staff stairs again, Jane still cursing the evil luck of encountering for the first time, in the way we had, someone with whom she would soon have a daily working relationship. To change the subject as we reached the ground floor, I remarked. 'I've been clearing up at home. I ought to be going over to the Recycling Complex.'

'*Are* you?' She seized on this as a very useful opportunity, and so I loaded into my boot, alongside my own junk, two weighty black bags of stuff discarded by the hotel: stripped wallpaper, lino squares, old beer mats, bar meal menus of the room as it would have been before the changes.

The matter of recognising and being recognised must have been still very much on my mind as I parked on the concrete forecourt of the Complex. Because I thought I knew its guardian, sitting in a tattered armchair beside his various skips and bins, despite his face being hidden behind the newspaper he was reading.

But how could I know him, know anything except that this was not the man I had seen working here on my last visit, several weeks ago?

There were containers for Household Rubbish, Garden Waste, Clear Glass, Coloured Glass, Saleable Clothing, Saleable Books,

Newspapers and Magazines. And the last two, with their mouths that snapped at your hands as you pushed your bushels of newsprint into them, reminded me of one of Geoff Stedman's dreams as related to me over a drink in the Drayhorse near the beginning of his last term in the Polytechnic.

Stedman was lying under some kind of transparent surface; perhaps glass or perspex, anyway he could see through it, and looking up at a crowd of familiar people, some of them celebrities excoriated in our 'fucking' conversations, others colleagues from the Polytechnic, all of them absolutely, stitchlessly naked. Neither Dennis Frostick nor myself featured, but Hulzer was there in the background, Reginald Torridge very prominently, and in the forefront Dave Underhill.

All of these people were eating – literally stuffing into their mouths, chewing and swallowing – piles of glossy magazine supplements and other pull-out-and-throw-away items from popular and broadsheet newspapers. And then defecating onto the glass surface, gradually covering it with a weight of ordure, so that Stedman felt he was being pressed to death with shit.

I switched off the engine, got out of the car, and unloaded the rubbish, mine and the hotel's, from the boot, swinging out the several black bags onto the ground beside the waste containers. The man in the armchair enjoying the unusual sunshine rustled his newspaper and looked round it. It was the sound, and the action, of someone yet again disturbed while trying to obtain a moment's peace.

'Nice if you'd showed me what it is you've brought before you dump it,' he said. Dropping his newspaper on his lap, raising his head so that his eyes could see me under the pulled-down peak of a tight green Council cap. Greg.

This was his new job, then. I froze with apprehension and didn't reply, cursing the malicious coincidence of meeting the black-bearded Greg in a situation like this. Then, to my relief, two more cars arrived to discharge their waste and at least we were not alone.

Without doing or saying anything to acknowledge acquaintance he insisted I show him the contents of each black bag before I hoisted them into the skip for Household Rubbish. My own junk he passed, grudgingly. But when I came to Jane's bags he fumbled among the scrolls of discarded wallpaper and found a batch of old menu cards.

'Can you read?' he enquired. This was a question I had never heard with pride or pleasure after the age of five. I ignored it, and tried to re-knot the mouth of the bag, thinking I would chuck it into the skip and have done with it. Greg pulled it out of my hands and re-tied the knot himself, dumping it onto the bonnet of my car. He pointed to a board attached to the wire fence of the Complex. 'It says NO TRADE WASTE,' he said.

'This isn't trade waste,' I began. But of course it was: shards of the former bar at the Clifftop Continental Hotel were discarded trade materials.

'You'll have to take those back if you don't want to pay a £5,000 fine.'

'Oh come on!'

But I flung them back in the boot, vowing that one day, in some small or large way, I would find a form of revenge applicable to this individual.

The opportunity came sooner than I expected, but so replete with ambiguities that it may not have counted as revenge at all.

✳

I restarted my jogging just after this; which means May, when you still, if you are sensible, wear a track suit against the chill breezes in these parts.

To my great pleasure I found in one of its breast-pockets, stored there in the previous summer, a five-pound note, four 50p coins and two 10p's, means of phoning for a taxi if I jogged too far and needed one, or sprained an ankle, or suffered anything worse (my name and address were on slip of paper in the same pocket.) As I plodded out on that bright and cool morning it was good to hear the coins and my keys jangling in the pocket, and know that I could still propel myself forward at this gentle, healthy pace without getting alarmingly breathless.

I pattered slowly down through the town and out to the place where fallen rocks under the cliffs shelved down at low tide to a point where the sand was flat and firm. When the waves had left wet corrugations of sand it was tough on the feet, but today my exercise surface was not bumpy, and conditions for a long leisurely run seemed generally excellent.

Above me now was the Lighthouse Museum, repaired and lately reopened for the summer season, and if I ran as far as the place where Jane's hotel marked the end of the cliffs and the beginning of the saltmarshes I would still have energy enough, I thought, to turn round and jog back. It would be a round trip of about three miles, not bad for the first jog of the year.

As I ran I thought that if, or perhaps when, Rosie came to live in the house in a couple of months' time, I could surely clear the unexpected undergrowth of my life in this town without too much trouble. The presence of Jane and Bill seemed to present no problems, perhaps even be an advantage. Jane could be relied upon to keep quiet about her connection with me in the past (and it hadn't been fully renewed, had it?) A matter like the animosity of Greg in regard to Flamingo would be no problem as long as I avoided him, and his seeing me around the place with another woman would help. That might even encourage Trevor Ridyard to stop showing his own inscrutable hostility.

Of course there was the difficulty of Rachel's possible continuation as a tenant of the top flat. But there had never been any potentially embarrassing relationship with Rachel (I'm sad to admit) and the house was quite large enough for Rosie and myself without using Rachel's quarters. There was also, as well as the agreeable knowledge that Rachel was still going to bed upstairs, a little rent accruing from her presence, though I would not care to reveal to Rosie *how* little.

Rachel would need to be introduced to Rosie (and for that matter, so would the Bramstons). As to the future, I myself should

140

prefer to go on living in this town, though Rosie might have different views. These were bridges to cross when one came to them. But everything seemed to be working out clearly and simply. I only had to make the firm decision about whether I readmitted Rosie permanently to my life.

I had reached the end of the cliffs and was level with the hotel. And I knew I had taken on too much on my first outing after a sedentary winter. My ribs ached, my knees were not supporting me as reliably as they had last summer. I felt my age suddenly. I knew I faced the humiliation of walking, or breathlessly stumbling, all the way back home from where I had reached if I carried on now. In short, I had to stop and rest. Well, I had cash in my pocket, and I'd heard from Jane that the theme bar was just opening, and there was the hotel at the top of the cliff steps. Which I accordingly mounted with some pain.

After washing and cooling down somewhat in the vestibule Gentlemen's, I limped into the Variety Bar (my dress being no infringement these days of any dress code in such places). I would take a drink to my window corner and keep out of sight just in case the Burgesses were already in evidence.

How rapidly and thoroughly the conversion had been accomplished! The little dais where the unused, long-untuned grand piano stood was now framed in a small mock-proscenium arch complete with red plasterboard curtains; it didn't make it a stage, but it set up theatrical associations. With the same intentions the repapered and repainted walls had been hung with dozens of signed black-and-white photographs of comedy and light musical entertainment artists, recurring among them depictions of Sid and Beryl Burgess at earlier stages of their careers. Bills advertising old shows flanked the bar counter.

And (I could not avoid him, because he smiled across at me the moment I entered) Sid Burgess himself, accoutred as smartly as always, stood behind it, marshalling glasses into neat squares in readiness for any lunchtime custom. Beside him, behind a lighted display of French rolls and butter, Scotch eggs and salads, quiches,

141

cold mackerel and 'Our Vegetarian Pie Options' was Beryl. They had come to this.

'Hul–lo! How are we today, young man?' Sid called out. Not seeing me other than as a stranger – I hoped – but treating me with the bonhomie of one who had served there for years greeting someone who had been a regular for just as long.

'Fine,' I said. 'I...' I was about to ask whether Mrs Bramston might be around, but decided I wouldn't; decided I would just order.

'Our official Gala opening is a week next Saturday,' Sid Burgess informed me. He ran through the names of several artists I had vaguely heard of (though not recently) whom he was certain would drop in for the occasion and be persuaded to do something. 'Watch this space. But we're running *ourselves* in from today. So what can I beguile you with...?'

It took me five seconds to realise that in his new capacity Sid was asking me for an order, not offering to take a request for a song. I looked round at the seating, all of it brand-new, imitation velvet chairs set at two-, four- and six-person tables. It was 11.45 a.m. I was his first customer ever in the Variety Bar. I asked for a Scotch.

He pushed the heavy little glass against the optic, obtaining the measure of whisky described in an honest little notice stuck on the mirror, turned round affably, plonked a cube of ice in it with tongs, gave a wide smile. And I realised – a sudden burst of revelation – that I *liked* Sid Burgess, very much. That warm, uncomplicated welcome convinced me that he either hadn't recognised me from the bedroom episode with Jane, or that he had and was prepared to forget it. Reassuring. It was puzzling, though (still harping on recognition?), that when I saw him at close quarters I noticed a resemblance to someone else, or perhaps more than one person, I could not name.

I chatted with him about the prospects for the Variety Bar. He assumed, very professional this, that I knew who he was. He talked about his stage life, dropped names he was quite entitled to drop, implied his and Beryl's celebrity as a prelude to saying that they had long anticipated this kind of job when they finally retired from haring up and down the country treading the boards.

142

But then he sighed, and leaned towards me confidentially (Beryl was now busying herself by walking around the tables seeing that everything was in order). Things could be a little hard these days for older artists, he told me quietly, so that 'retirement' to one very pleasant place, to work on a scheme of this kind while he and Beryl still had the strength, seemed a very nice option. Besides, 'to be philosophical', he was an advocate of settling for what you could get.

'But then I'm fifty-eight,' he declared. I was touched to be receiving these confessions, except that I believed he was several, even many, years older than that, much older than me, hardly less than seventy. 'Are you telling me that any of us ever do much better at my time of life? In entertainment? In business, these days? In politics – or in love?' He laughed, and I found myself nodding ruefully; his expression didn't suggest a hint about anything. 'As for *sport* – you're finished at *twenty*-eight. What do *you* do?' I told him fast what I had done, to disperse any faint recall of that bedroom, that video. Sid nodded understandingly, smiled, said nothing. Lecturers were not a breed he often encountered.

Then, God knows why, but perhaps it was his references to settling for what you could get, to love, to being fifty-eight, I began in the empty Variety Bar to recite to Sid Burgess what I myself planned to do now; that is, marry a handsome widow rather younger than myself, whom I'd known for some time, who had considerable savings of her own and had been prepared to allow me a year to make up my mind, which was how I had come to live here (and she had the thighs of a handsome air hostess, I thought, without speaking that detail aloud.)

He listened to it all with apparent absorption and sympathy. But I was suddenly embarrassed at revealing so much in answer to his own confessions. So to please him, I said, 'By the way, I came to your show in the Horizon Theatre just before Christmas. I really enjoyed it.'

'Yes, I realised you were there. No doubt inveigled into it by one of my nieces?'

I stared. I was silenced. Sid looked a mite uncertain as he

smiled. Did he think he might have made a mistake?

'You weren't numerous, either of those evenings,' he added. 'You were in the audience with my niece Kathryn the first night, weren't you? About the tenth row of the stalls?'

'Kathryn?'

'*Katie* she likes to be called.'

'Katie! Yes, of course – Rachel.'

'Kathryn Rachel. My niece. The Tillinghursts. Her mother, on the piano – my youngest sister, Maisie Burgess. Between us – no, *strictly* between us – she should never have married Jack Tillinghurst. An impractical dreamer who was never going to do anything. Wanted to write books, but well – you know... *Never marry out of the profession!*'

Slowly I said (still thinking of how that might apply to myself and Rosie), 'But how can you remember one face in a dark theatre one night of a tour, even if it's next to your niece's?'

'Oh I can remember most of the audience at our farewell performance. Eighteen of you, I think there were? Up to the interval. Fourteen after. Twelve of those were comps.'

'Then you didn't continue with the tour?'

'We didn't *have* a tour. We hoped for one, but nobody answered our agent's phone calls. Maisie set up the nights at the Horizon, out of the kindness of her heart. No one at all came the following evening. Christmas, you know! You were our last ever patrons. Oh, we took a good look at the firing squad that night, I can assure you.'

'I can't believe it.'

He was delighted with my comment.

'Well then, *don't.* I'd like that. Don't talk this all round the town, though, will you! I know you won't.' He had shocked himself with this candid excursion; I had shocked myself with mine. Was there a couple of seconds of fear in his eyes, fear that he had trusted me with too much?'

'I won't. Never in all my life,' I assured him.

He believed me, shifted along the bar to greet his second, third and fourth customers, trippers coming in as if it was not a novelty on

144

which the Burgesses' life depended but something that had always existed; unsurprised and incurious people.

When he was free again he rang for a taxi for me. Outside, I waited in pelting rain for it for fifteen minutes, and back in the house I stripped off my well-meaning jogging clothes to sink my miserably aching old limbs in a hot bath.

✳

The same rain went on, every day it seemed, well into June. And took me back to June last year, to a memory which raised my spirits during a few wet days of doubting whether I had made the right decision about Rosie.

Dennis Frostick's amateur prediction about the damp patch on the Games Field was correct, but it was proved to be so too late for Stedman's dutiful reporting of it to matter. If he had not already been given notice of his redundancy it wouldn't have helped. He had known better than Dr Hulzer and Dr Torridge. They resented that. Unusually for examination time (when the weather is often perfect, sometimes the summer's only two weeks of sunshine) it had rained hard in the days coming up to the written paper for the Auxiliary Modules exams. The night before, though, the rain had stopped and today there was a wan, grudging sunlight shining on the rows of students at their exam desks in the ground floor hall of the Annexe.

These were Catering and Catering Management candidates, plus large numbers of young men and women I had never met, sitting a paper devised by a central board. They covered almost every sort of Main Option, from Commercial Studies to Advanced Marketing to Business German, for which you needed to know nothing of Goethe or Heine or Rilke or Günter Grass, or even Bismarck or Hitler. Three duty invigilators were in charge, Reginald Torridge, Dennis Frostick, and myself.

At five to ten the sun went in. The candidates were twenty-five minutes into the paper. The atmosphere in the hall was warm and

145

oppressive, unrelieved by the fact that the double door into the foyer was open, as was the farther door from the foyer into the car park. Beyond the car park, of course, was the Games Field.

A girl sitting at the very front facing the open doors suddenly exclaimed 'Oh look!' Very quietly, not to disturb the dead silence of serious effort in the hall. Almost as if speaking to herself. But when she caught my eye she pointed her pen at the doors, so I did look. Torridge was patrolling at the back of the room, but Frostick was coming slowly down one of the aisles and joined me to watch what was happening outside. The ground beyond the parked cars was no longer the fresh green of the early summer grass but the dull grey hue of a flood. Already we could see water advancing quite quickly under the vehicles and lapping their wheels, spreading over the entire concrete surface of the car park. I ran out to the outer door. The flood was rapidly rippling towards us.

Why didn't I try to shut the door at that moment? I don't know. What I do know is that I returned to tell Torridge, and by the time he reached the door he was unable to close it; by then the force of the flood was too strong for him. The water was two or three inches deep in the foyer, and the Deputy Director couldn't close the inner doors either. In aghast indecision he stood at the front looking severely over the heads of the rows of students, all of whom, had by now seen what was taking place. Something like a wavelet hit his ankles.

Frostick was quick to claim his triumph of prophecy. 'What did I tell you!' was written joyously all over his face as the tide reached him. Too late for his shoes, but to save his trousers, he pulled off footwear and socks and rolled trouser-legs up to his knees to stand bare-footed in the dirty water. I did the same. Along the rows of desks the candidates were now openly talking, exclaiming and laughing nervously. Torridge irrelevantly called for 'Silence!'

'Geoff Stedman warned us about this last autumn,' I said, provocatively I hoped, looking at items of dreck coming in on the wavelets and thinking that Geoff would appreciate the symbolism of a flood of rubbish engulfing the Polytechnic. Torridge took no notice of me. That remark could not have helped my own reputation.

146

Exasperation, fear, bewildered hesitation had taken over the president of the Ballroom Dancing Society.

The waters were rising under the chairs, the students were awkwardly lifting their feet off the floor and trying to think where to rest them. At the same time they wrote faster, because they were conscious that they had already lost several minutes. One by one, feet came up to seat level, with candidates sitting in clumsy yogic positions or painfully cross-legged on chairs only large enough for bottoms, raised higher above sheets on which they wrote in precariously stooped postures. Some found that effort impossible, and kicked off their shoes, putting them on the desks. And just dipped their feet back into the grey inundation.

'They can't continue,' Frostick declared. 'We'll have to call it off.'

'We have no authority to invalidate the examination,' Torridge asserted. He was now paddling up to his soaked trouser-shins, having refused to roll up the legs. 'I'll inform Management.'

But Torridge *was* Management. And not even Management had any power to hold back the tide. Nevertheless the Deputy Director sloshed his way self-importantly to a telephone in the Reception office, whose inhabitants were perched on their desks in despair, having rung the fire brigade. He returned with an instruction from the Director that the students should carry on, the rescue services having been informed.

'Please continue the examination,' he called out. 'Please continue everyone. It's just a flash flood. Quiet, *please!*'

A brackish smell, as of rotting leaves or damp upholstery, filled the place. Rubbish had drifted in on the surface of the flood, in particular a green-striped condom which washed along under chairs and somehow described a circle to end in front of Torridge, standing by the desk at the front. I noticed that both the acoustic and the temperature had altered, that Torridge was calling out to the students across the chilly skin of a lake which had substantially cooled the hall, so that shirtsleeved students resumed their coats and cardigans.

And surely it would become dangerous if the water went on rising? All the laughter and chatter had ceased. There was now an

147

uneasy quiet, many faces looking intent and afraid. Through it we could hear the soft lap of liquid against the walls.

Torridge's maintenance of dignity was in fact undignified, a comedy of pomposity, the demeanour of a man who had taken himself too seriously for so long that he was capable of no other reaction. Afterwards, students said that Dr Torridge had been prepared to go down with the Polytechnic and take them with him. For many long minutes people assumed that he would be forced to let them go if water reached seat level and above, and still went on rising. But then fate came, undeservedly, to Torridge's assistance.

Suddenly the water was seen to be not rising any further. A matchstick carried in on its surface had reached a small existing stain on a wall near where I stood, but failed to be lifted above that. The tide was not going to cover the mark, it remained steady. Not ebbing, but not flowing either. And eventually, completing the paper as best they could and stopping on the dot at Torridge's instruction, the students shuffled their efforts into neat piles of paper and we waded down the rows to collect them.

Once they were outside they made at once for the stairs up to the refectory. Echoes of hysterical laughter came down to us. We checked and counted the scripts and gazed at the dirty lagoon that had been the examination hall. Dennis Frostick was radiant with satisfaction. Not knowing that I had already spoken about this, he said to Torridge, 'I do recall Mr Stedman sending in a memo about water on the field. Is it still on file somewhere?'

Torridge turned a furious look on him and barked, 'Yes! You don't have to repeat all that,' evidently forgetting that it was I who had mentioned it two hours earlier.

'They would *not* listen!' Frostick said later. 'Serve the copulators right.'

Until the end he maintained that the morning had been the high point of his Polytechnic career.

✳

When I met Bill Bramston in the Co-op Superstore one Sunday early in June I realised that I hadn't actually seen Jane's husband since Christmas, only kept in touch with his activities through her; mostly his illicit camera and video work at that. I'd been to their home alone with Jane several times, met her, intentionally and cautiously, out of doors (also accidentally; this town is a small place), visited the hotel and seen her, including on the day we saw Bill's video. But I had not run into Bill. Only heard his voice curtly handing me on to Jane when I'd unavoidably needed to phone her at home.

Bill was pushing his trolley in my direction and must have seen me before I saw him. Then he was gazing uncertainly at banks of fruit and vegetables, shopping list in hand. I carried merely a small wire basket for my modest requirements. I saw Bill pause, and put out a hand to feel and appraise three grapefruit, all of which he laid in the trolley. Then he took down four green bananas and eyed them sadly.

I approached him, a little surprised that he had not greeted me yet. 'How goes it?'

He looked at me as if he had not recognised me. At first. Then he continued to stare as if I was unknown to him, though without the surprise or curiosity of someone addressed in a public place by an apparent stranger. He did not add the four bananas to the pile of goods in his trolley but held them at waist level pointed towards me, in a hand that trembled. I could have imagined that he meant to do me harm with them.

'Is all this business with my wife anything to do with you?' he asked. Meaninglessly, in a low, toneless, yet threatening voice. I had never seen the correct, dull, courteous Bill Bramston in such a mood, or heard him use these smouldering tones.

'Business?' I thought, without saying that. Recently the only 'business' I had had with Jane would have been the few frustrated moments while watching the video on the bed in the hotel. All I said was, 'With me? What...?' And I smiled, probably a false and uneasy smile. Were all the people in this town paranoid? What had I been known or seen to do that would reduce me, in Bill's book, to 'you'?

Surely Jane would not have told him anything.

Bill seemed not to have heard or grasped my question in the busy store, or else he refused to hear it. Did my genuine confusion reassure him? At any rate he dropped the bananas into the trolley and relaxed.

'I'm sorry, Mike', he murmured, looking embarrassed. Or worse than embarrassed: ashamed. 'I'm probably being a fool. When can you come round for a meal?'

'That's all right,' I said pointlessly, admitting by the phrase that there might have been something he could have accused me of. 'Come for a meal? Any time.. It's been a while. How are you keeping? How *is* Jane?'

A nervous mistake. All his uneasiness returned.

'Jane?... Fine! ... I'll be ringing. Bye.'

✳

Although my decision had been unexpectedly made in the Variety Bar several days before, I am a bad letter writer and I still hadn't clinched it in a letter to Rosie.

I sat in the dining room at the polished table, and, to confirm myself in my resolve, sat with the Christmas air hostess photograph in front of me. I had been glad, I wrote, to give her some thoughts about how we should live if we did finally agree on getting together. But it now seemed to me that there would be no harm in an earlier resolution of our affairs, seeing that so many practical matters required to be settled. We had discussed some of those already, why didn't we just say now that we *would* be living together when our year apart expired in August, and go into all these matters as things fully settled, rather than hypothetical arrangements?

I rewrote this missive twice, then sat and re-read the final version many times. It was hot. The house was silent. The street was silent. Summer did not lessen the loneliness I felt when, as today, a Saturday, I could not reasonably ring up Jane. It was still open to me

150

not to post the letter. But at six o'clock I went out and did just that.

By return of post Rosie signified that she was full of delight to know of the decision my words made clear. She would certainly arrive on the date in August I suggested. She would like some directions for reaching me nearer the time. Meanwhile, could she please have my phone number so that we could actually speak again after this long interval?

Which might effectively have brought me a sense of relief and purpose and security.

✳

Geoff Stedman's revenge was drastic and colourful.

'Ultimately I have fucking Torridge to thank for being redundant,' he said. 'He needn't have gone along with Underhill as readily as he did. I have *both* of those fuckers to thank, for their separate contributions. And that I intend to do. Most sincerely. Now. They're both busy elsewhere at the moment.'

Torridge and Underhill were, in this slack end-of-term period, attending a management course on another site of the Polytechnic. Geoff looked at his watch and blinked.

'They could be back very soon – I gather their course ends with a management lunch. I shall show my gratitude to them at once, if I can. Before they get back.'

I still don't know whether Stedman had a particular plan in mind at that point. I do know that I feared whatever he might do, and tried to warn him, in case it proved destructive as well as ingenious.

'It's not worth it, Geoff,' I said.

'It might be.'

I did not like the sound of that.

We crossed the car park, where the combined enterprise of several local charities had placed collection and recycling containers for the end-of-year clear-out. Students and staff could fill them with unwanted paper, bottles, clothing, books for resale.

Anything else, See the Attendant, who had a special van for larger, more valuable items.

Stedman guided me past the bins, in through the main door, over to the lift, in which he pressed the button for the fourth floor. I went with him; to restrain him if necessary, though I later wondered if my presence actually provided encouragement.

We stepped out of the lift nearer to Underhill's door, but Geoff grimly said, 'Torridge first!' and turned left.

Torridge's corridor overlooked a narrow purposeless courtyard where the caretaker had cultivated a small decorative garden: rockery, plants in tubs, a pond with waterlilies and goldfish. The day was so hot that every sash window along here was open.

Two-twenty. Through its own open windows we could see that the refectory, two floors down on the other side of the courtyard, was empty at this hour on a Friday after Finals, one third of the students having already left, and teaching staff gone home or away for the week-end. We could see cleared and wiped tables, shining. No sounds came up to us.

Strangely, everyone still trusted each other enough to let most doors stay unlocked. Torridge's door was even slightly open. Geoff knocked softly, and waited. Knocked again, put his head into the gap and sang 'Dr Torridge, sir!' in an ominous counter-tenor.

Still no answer. Satisfied Reginald Torridge was not inside, Stedman flung back the door hard against the wall, stood framed in the gap, and shouted, in a vibrant baritone, 'Torridge, your hour is at hand!'

The room, in contrast to Underhill's, was aggressively neat, a staid, featureless place, very much an office and not a study. There were few books, just a couple of piles of photocopied documents, shelves of box files fastidiously labelled on their spines, stark Polytechnic armchairs never humanised by informal use. There was one picture. Almost paradoxically appropriate, it was of an old white carthorse in a pasture, 'Faithful's Reward'. Torridge was incapable of humour and I took this to be a retained family relic.

There were wall-cupboards, and the door of one stood open. And why should his room door also be open? Had Torridge been back from lunch already? I was deeply alarmed in case he should turn up again and find us here.

Inside this cupboard, at eye-level, were stacked-up files, packets of A4 paper, jars of glue, a heavy-duty stapler, a rolled-up something secured with a rubber band, all designated 'STATIONERY'. Immediately above this was a shelf labelled 'BALLROOM DANCING SOCIETY'.

'Ah hah! What have we here?' Stedman exclaimed. I realised he had chanced on something symbolising everything he despised in Torridge and in the Polytechnic. His hands gently lifted down a pile of tapes on old-fashioned reel-to-reel spools. 'We shall have a ticker-tape display,' he said. ' "Great Days of Dancing"? ' He was reading from Torridge's home-made label. 'Pirated from an LP no doubt. Naughty.'

He moved out into the corridor and dropped all these tapes onto a ledge under an open window.

'You *can't*,' I protested. But he loosened the end of one tape.

'First Movement: Andante,' he announced. And holding the tape-end, he cast the plastic spool down and out into the courtyard, where it landed with a clatter. He took a second tape, went to a second window. 'Second Movement: Lento.' With a slower motion he spun the second spool down onto the concrete. Each tape hung down like a shiny streamer from where he attached it to the handle on the window. 'Finale: Tarantella!'

I gave up arguing in horrified despair as Stedman disposed of the rest of the tapes, window by window, in the same fashion. But I grabbed at his arm and protested when he revisited Torridge's room and reappeared carrying a six-inch high collection of bakelite 78s, music of Torridge's earliest years in charge of the Polytechnic Ballroom Dancing Society; which he had, after all, started as a student over forty years ago.

'Careful, careful!' he chided me; and elbowed his way past. Daintily he set the records down beside one open window.

'Geoff, *no!*' I laid both my hands flat down on top of the 78s.

153

'This is vandalism.'

'This is defending standards,' he replied.

'They'd only have sentimental value.'

'I hope so.'

'You *mustn't*!'

But I eventually removed my hands from the records. And I felt my lips smiling at Stedman's absurd audacity. I had no time for Torridge either. Not since that heart-to-heart we had had about my 'friendships' with complaining women students. Another story...

For a moment Geoff seemed to agree with my last plea, and hesitated.

'Well, as a concession to our friendship, I shall restrict it to just this pile.' What he had carried out represented about half of the bakelite discs I had seen on the cupboard shelf. 'And I shall lob them through those windows over there. To give them a chance – someone might be there to catch them.' He read the label on the first record. 'How nice! "Amapola: Quick step." Fucking Victor Sylvester and his Orchestra.'

Seemingly without aiming, and as if casting a quoit or a frisby, he sent the disc spinning and gliding down across the courtyard into the nearest opposite window of the refectory. We heard the sound of it smashing, and the echo of that sound in the empty hall. I expected some reaction, shouts of alarm, or consternation, or protest. None came. Presumably the kitchen staff had also all left. Everything stayed eerily still, as if inviting another fracture of the peace. '"The Anniversary Waltz". One anniversary Torridge will not be repeating,' Stedman declared. Crash. ' "Jealousy: Tango." ' Crash.

He went along the corridor with the black, red-labelled discs cradled in the crook of his left arm, sowing them through each of the refectory windows two floors below: Geraldo, Harry Roy, Joe Loss, fox-trots, *rumbas, pasa dobles*. Were there twenty, thirty in all? Fewer, probably. But it seemed like more. I waited in terror for someone to appear and blame me as much as Geoff for this.

'Of these we cannot speak,' he said in conclusion. He was holding a clutch of unlabelled plastic-cased small cassette tapes.

'Thereof we shall be silent.' He dropped them one by one accurately into the goldfish pond.

We left that corridor and walked back across the landing where the lift was. The lift doors opened scarily as soon as we reached it, but to my relief they only revealed the volunteer attendant of the charity bins, carrying a large cardboard box. Did the sight of that actually give Stedman his next idea?

'Before you fill that, can you quickly take some things for me? I'm in rather a hurry,' he said. 'I don't have my keys with me, but I may have left my door open.'

When he tried the handle, Dave Underhill's door opened, and Dave was not inside, a stroke of luck releasing Stedman from the necessity of giving convoluted explanations. We entered this dis-ordered den with its pop posters and hard plastic chairs with Geoff saying, 'Yes, if you can manage to take a few things I'll soon sort some out for you.'

'Geoff – ' I said. But behind the young attendant's back Stedman raised a finger to his lips.

I believe that either the sight of volumes more suitable for Stedman's purpose, or fear that there would not be space enough in the box, saved Underhill's small collection of slim volumes of recent verse, editions published by Chatto and Windus, or Faber and Faber, or Shanks and Armitage. But while Dave's computer screen relayed kaleidoscopic patterns Stedman lifted down and rolled up posters of the Stones, Mike Oldfield, Deep Purple, the Shit Factor and others, and made a fast selection of books for the collector's box. He spoke only to me. 'Lacan? Foucault? I think we can dispense with those. "Sixties Kings of Rock" – old hat now, I'm afraid. Stanley Fish? Belsey? They'll find good homes, I'm sure.' This way about fifteen of Underhill's collection went to nearby charity shops. 'I shall miss some of them, but it's in a good cause.'

Then he stopped and stared in deep meditation at the images whirling on the computer screen.

'Look – would you have space for that?' he asked the young man.

I could not believe this. The collector could not believe it either.

'What? The Macintosh?'

Stedman nodded.

'Geoff, I won't let you.' I knew that this computer was not the property of the Polytechnic but Underhill's own.

'Well, I've been wondering for months if I could bring myself to let it go. They're getting so sophisticated now. And I've got something smarter on order. What would I do with both?'

'Geoff – this is a several hundred pound job,' I pleaded with him, guessing.

'Oh *more*,' Stedman mused. 'Still, if you could use it?' The young man's face was alight with incredulous gratitude. 'Unplug it and take it, then. Before I change my mind.'

'I refuse to let you do this, Geoff,' I declared. The young man was already winding the flex into a reel. 'Please – I'll have it myself.' But Stedman merely laughed, and helped to fit the computer into the box. It made a heavy load but the charity volunteer was strong and able to cope with it, Stedman keeping the lift doors open and downstairs assisting him to hoist the box into his van.

When we turned round from this task we saw Torridge and Underhill. They were about a hundred yards away across the field, walking around its periphery with heads down in deep after-lunch discussion and coming towards us. There was no reason to think we had been seen.

'Let's wait for them,' Stedman suggested. I wanted to hurry both of us to my car and make an escape before we were spotted. But Stedman's hunch was that if we avoided them and were noticed it would cast suspicion on us concerning what had happened in their rooms.

When they reached us, still in quiet conference,

'Dr Torridge – Reginald!' Stedman exclaimed warmly; and, with a nod of acknowledgement to Underhill, 'Do you think I might have a brief word?' He touched Torridge gently on the forearm.

Torridge had no idea what to do. Geoff's tones must have been a shock, the use of 'Reginald' would have sounded unusual, a challenge. Torridge had used 'Geoff' as superior to inferior, but hardly anyone in the Polytechnic used a first name in addressing the Deputy Director.

'Why yes, Mr Stedman,' he now answered; in a guarded way.

'It's about the unpleasant duty you and Dave – Mr Underhill – were obliged to carry out in respect of myself.'

Torridge looked blank, as if the affair of Geoff's redundancy had gone out of his mind. But when Stedman went on, rapidly, his expression changed to one of earnest, if condescending, attention.

'You did not want to have to inform me that I was surplus to requirements,' Geoff said. 'You did not enjoy having to do it. But seeing that circumstances outside your control compelled you to do it, at least you did it with grace and compassion, and I'm grateful for that.'

Torridge's eyes sharpened for just a moment of speculation as to whether Stedman was mocking him. But I am sure that Geoff's buried irony was beyond his discerning, the well-acted warmth in his tone allowing him to assume that the man was sincere. Geoff kept up his front by playing on Torridge's vanity and self-regard; Underhill could do nothing without questioning his superior's perception of the situation.

'It could have been done in so much worse a way,' Stedman continued, 'but I'm happy to say that because of the sympathy with which you did it, I shall not leave the Polytechnic with any sense of bitterness. None whatsoever.'

I came near to prayer in my hoping that Stedman would not go on too long, or try to pull this one on Underhill as well. But he did neither. It was achievement enough to have excavated the tiny nugget of guilt in Torridge's feelings about his departure.

'Mr Stedman – Geoff – you can't imagine how much I appreciate what you have just expressed,' he said slowly. I saw Geoff's lower lip tremble at that, and his eyes become dangerously bright. But,

'Well, thank you, Reginald,' he said, putting out a hand.

'Thank you, Geoff,' Torridge replied, taking it. And Underhill gave an uncomfortable, penetrating smile as we walked away.

All I could manage to say was, when they could not hear us, 'Are you here on Monday?' There was only one last winding-down week of term to go.

'I hope to be on a Greek island on Monday.'

He never managed it. I shall come to that.

✷

Receiving my number, Rosie began phoning and phoning about the practical details of her arrival; and invariably chose difficult moments. Her very first call interrupted some Saturday morning jogging plans.

After my initial chastening attempt after the winter to resume regular exercise (when I collapsed, took a drink in the Variety Bar, and concluded, with Sid Burgess's help, that I did need Rosie to support my ageing structures), I set myself more modest targets. Every three days, weather permitting, I drove to a suitable starting point, made a short round trip, returned to the car, and drove home.

I was garbed in the track suit with my car keys in my hand, and leaving the house, when the phone rang.

'After so long, we talk!' Rosie declared, after my short 'Hullo.'

'We more than talk,' I replied, at once regretting my stupidly inapppropriate abruptness – who else would it be but Rosie calling? As she chattered I looked at her photograph, now pinned to the wall above the telephone, and I really did look forward to the physical reality.

'Oh yes, we certainly do talk. It's only three weeks now, isn't it – three weeks tomorrow, Sunday, yes – I'd like to make it around five, if we could, I've a lot of things to deal with earlier in the day. I've got to –' And she began on a long explanatory list of details and a series of questions about household matters which I would have preferred to leave to her. 'I've a lot of stuff to bring. You know I have an estate car now? Oh of course, you wouldn't know that, but I do. I just have to hope everything goes into it. I think it will. I suppose you wouldn't feel able to come over yourself and – I can't ask you to do that, I'll manage somehow, don't worry. What you *can* do is give me some idea of the size of the rooms in the house, and the windows. Could you do some measuring, and I'll ring you again to-morrow?'

Which she did. And the day after. I began to accept that our joint tenure of this house, permanent or only temporary, would require a number of additions and changes, and sessions of work of a kind I had never put in. When I tried to refer to how and why we had finally taken our momentous step, Rosie always bore me away from the subject on a wave of mundane considerations. There would be plenty of time to go into all that later, she assured me. Keys, security locks, the state of the cooking equipment, the carpets, the lampshades were more important for the moment.

But I would be enthralled to see her, I was certain of that.

When she had finished I drove down to a parking place about a quarter of a mile from an agreeably quiet part of the beach. My planned route followed from there a public footpath skirting an orchard, passed through a coppice, crossed a bridge of planks over a stream (with a steel rail to cling to), took me up onto a bank beside a long reed-covered channel, and finally led down over the dunes to the sands.

It had seemed a calm day when I set out. But in the coppice, as I walked beside a dry ditch filled with last autumn's foliage, a strong breeze began to fling branches of saplings and high bushes against my head. I saw the pale green, almost white undersides of tormented summer leaves flash against the unbroken blue of the sky. When I reached the empty, open expanses of the beach a strong offshore wind was raising eddies of white sand to sting my hands and face.

Any holiday families hoping for restful sunshine hours here had already given up on the morning. The force of the wind rearranged the sandgrains in small whirlwinds up the dunes and between them. Every gap formed a funnel through which the hot, stinging particles were driven. Peculiar weather.

I persisted nevertheless. I had come to jog, and I was going to do that. In a sheltered hollow of the dunes, out of the wind and far from any of the few figures still on the beach, I stripped off the track suit and set off to run in my swimming shorts. I faced the wind first, with the idea that it would carry me back more easily when I turned. And I found I was plodding towards a pair of human dots: a black one standing on the shoreline three hundred yards away, a lighter one out among the waves, swimming.

Running along the firm sand at the water's edge towards them I grimly realised that the one standing by the water was Greg.

The following wind carried tiny sounds of clashing music in the summer Amusements Park back on the esplanade, well over a mile away, a breezy fair organ competing with heavy rock rhythms. Above this, it was not behind me but ahead, came a single voice crying out. A light, distressed crying. It was the swimmer in the water. I recognised her, with sheer disbelief at first and then a momentary anger at being deceived about her whereabouts, as Rachel.

For all the wind, the sea was quiet. The tide was ebbing, I guessed; its ripples had each time, as I ran beside them, been drawing back a little farther, like courtiers retreating while making obeisances, water respecting earth. 'Help me, Help me...' called the yellow head twenty yards out.

Repeated. Repeated. 'Help me! '

Greg and I came face to face and knew each other. At once we both looked at Rachel in the water. In horror. 'She's in trouble,' I said breathlessly, panting. 'Can't you...?' Greg's reaction was – wasn't it? – bewildered despair. He was fully-clothed – well, in jeans and T-shirt only, not even his black sweater to pull off. I was in the swimming trunks. He made some sort of despairing gesture with his hands. In these seconds a dreadful memory came back of a passage in Rachel's autobiography: one day, she feared, she would swim out too far to have the strength to swim back...

'Help her!' I shouted blankly at Greg. I ran forward into the water and expected Greg to strip off and wade out faster than I could. He did not move. All he did was walk out a few paces to where the waves covered his trainers, and say – and I couldn't believe him – 'I can't swim.'

'Help me!'

No one else for hundreds of yards along the beach. In the distance only a couple of unreachable families paddling, the wind billowing in their shirts. Rachel's hand waving from the water, vanishing under it. A head still bobbing, above the surface, disappearing, reappearing. 'Help me!' 'I *can't*, I *can't*,' Greg repeated. I waded out farther myself, willing the sea to push Rachel nearer so that I could grab her when it was no higher than my waist.

It didn't; and besides, the tall Rachel could have stood up in it herself where I was standing

The water was now touching the bottom of my ribs, moving more forcefully here as I splashed desperately towards her. She was still yards and yards away, where it was deep and treacherous. Already it was threatening to bear me off my feet.

I would have to stop wading and start swimming. When I turned my head pleadingly for a final appeal to Greg I saw him still in the shallows, agitated and anguished in his gestures, but speechless. I swallowed water, and salt stinged my eyes, as I propelled myself off my feet. In the purest terror. And breast-stroked towards Rachel. I had not lost all my breath in jogging, and found just enough to strike out forward, aware with unexampled fear that I could no longer put a foot down and touch sand. It was myself and lurching water. A tide pulling me outwards. Nothing else.

My eyes looked at a restless infinity of blue. When had the horizon ever been just a straight, secure line? I only saw death out here, in dark and cold undulations ruffled by the wind with the sun glintingly reflected on them. Infinity. I knew death as the mouthfuls I tried to spit out as I strained back my head and aching neck to stay above the water and reach Rachel.

I suppose that by then I was actually swimming, testing my father's first maxim about the width of a swimming bath that could save you in an emergency. Because Rachel was nearer now. 'Help me.' The voice was lower, quieter, no need for it to call or shout. And suddenly I had reached her. But how could I turn now, get hold of her, bear her back out of danger? Her waving hand brushed my arm. Brushed it again. And held it.

I tried to shake off this hand, fearing that if I gripped it we might claw each other down. I found myself unable to. And then I was unbelievably turned over on my back and half-rotated, ending up at right-angles to the beach. Rachel had somehow got two hands hard round my waist, and 'Float!' she commanded, turning me farther round so that my eyes saw the unresting horizon once more, and I was starting my one other swimming stroke, certainly floating now, on my back. Had Rachel actually life-saved *me*?

'It's all right – now,' she gasped. Yes, I was swimming on my back, kicking out with my legs, brushing water aside in wide half-circles with my hands and arms, half floating, half-swimming gradually back to the shallows with Rachel similarly swimming beside me, sometimes putting out a hand to touch me and reassure herself. Endlessly I jerked and circled my exhausted legs, paddled with my hands. Until I felt my feet and back grating on sand and I saw Rachel rise to stand up alongside me in shin-deep ripples. Except that it was not Rachel but Flamingo.

I stayed sitting down in the water as she wiped her pale face and wrung out her hair, which in the water had looked like her sister's shorter cut. We made the strangest trio, I thought, generous-hearted from sheer relief: the very tall girl shivering and tense all the way up her elegant body, raising her right knee (beautifully bending the whole incomparable limb) and kicking out with her foot to lose the last of the cramp; Greg looking stricken with shame; myself recumbent and shattered in the warm water here, staring up at both. Then Flamingo broke down and cried. And bent down and kissed me.

'What were you doing?' was all she wailed to Greg, in tones of utter, almost snarling, contempt.

'I thought you'd been in the navy,' I said, thinking I would lose nothing by that.

'Did you, then,' was his reply. After that no one said anything else. At all.

My main feeling was one of achieved revenge. Proving my father's second legend about swimming, I had shown up Greg for

162

what he unquestionably was: a very good stalker (he had been watching Flamingo's movements whenever he could and discovered her regular bathing spot) but the case of a sailor unable to swim. He must be feeling a deeper humiliation, in front of Flamingo/Vicki than any he had inflicted on me. I was glad of that.

And then a stranger thought occurred, and overwhelmed me. What if Greg *could* swim? What if his anguish at the sight of Flamingo crying out for help in the sea had been assumed when he saw me. And what if letting Flamingo drown was to have been his ghastly revenge for her rejecting him? And seeing a reasonable chance of getting me drowned as well, he took it? Because I did find it hard to convince myself that Greg was incapable of swimming; although, if he could in fact swim, not to have struck out to save Flamingo would have been an inconceivable relinquishment of his pride, an acceptance of two persons' lasting contempt if they survived, and an act which would bring profound suspicion down on his head.

Flamingo, recovered, walked away towards the dunes where, I now saw, a small pile of bright clothing nestled. Greg watched her go, but did not follow. Finally, without any further word, he wandered off slowly along the shoreline, not looking back. Flamingo soon emerged dressed, saw that he had gone, and waved to me, calling out 'Good-bye.' When I was sure that there was enough space between the two of them for her to get away safely, I turned and walked (I didn't jog) back to the car.

✳

Dear Mike,

Hullo, how are you? I'm feeling really sorry I haven't been in touch while I've been away and when Vicki wrote and told me how brave you had been thinking you would rescue her from the sea I thought I must write and let you know what has been happening.

It's been great here, which – the picture, and the photos of me in my best hay harvest outfit will give you an idea of it – is a really nice place [she was wearing a bikini and sunglasses and standing in the middle of a mown field]. *It's called Wagley Farm, and is the headquarters of something called NEWS, which stands for New Environmental Writing Scheme. I read about it in a list in the Library of places you could go in groups to do writing courses. The idea is, you sign up for a stay of four weeks when there is a lot of farm work to be done, and you help the farmer for half the day and get experience of what it is to be close to nature and soil so that it improves the writing you do and assists in giving town people a better feeling for the environment at the same time. The farmer herself is a poet, Mrs Jill Jardine, and our work in the fields picking strawberries and raspberries and other fruit is how we pay for the tuition she gives us in writing poems. We also help sell fruit on her roadside stalls, which I like to think I am rather good at because people stop for me.*

Seriously, I have started to write a lot of poetry and Jill believes it is good and I am improving all the time, also getting a sense of nature into my writing, which I think it needed. I am very eager to let you see it, and will come down and show you some of the things I've done as soon as I return, which seems likely to be in August as I've signed up for another four-week course here. Also it will be good to see you once more, though I am sure you won't have missed me when seeing Vicki (she quite likes you, do you know that...!)

Anyway, see you soon,

Love,

Rachel xxxxx

Five kisses. There would have been a time when Rachel's letter would have given me pause, had me thinking about what possibilities it suggested, how I might build on it. Now it was too late for that, I told myself.

Had I been unconsciously grateful for the solitude that would end when Rosie joined me here? My last days alone felt valuable, my last opportunities to go somewhere, do something, by my own choice alone. I sat in the car watching the sea one evening, at that same vantage point from which I had surveyed the town and considered my future on an afternoon last August, returning from the city having picked up my new spectacles from Dr Koning. I was now a year older and substantially more resolved. I would not let Rachel's letter, I was emphatic about it, raise any ridiculous hopes or dreams.

Rachel had never acknowledged my letter, either still lying unseen (wedged under a mat perhaps?) at the foot of the indoor stairs or read and ignored. It would seem she expected to return and live in the top flat, as before, and I would have to pass her off to Rosie as a harmless long-term tenant. But nothing would stop me using the next day to indulge, before Rosie came next week, my own individual freedom by driving off somewhere, anywhere to enjoy the lustrous summer weather alone.

Duly, by eight-thirty next morning, as if it could have known about my intention, the entire world had gone sultry and misty, vindictively determined to ruin my plans. I nearly abandoned the idea, but I didn't. I tried the air outside the house, found it was no worse than muggy, believed the sun would be shining after an hour or two, and set out. I just didn't care where I ended up, had a pub lunch, walked in a lane or on a beach, pleased myself.

I soon tired of the volume of traffic on the main coast road, every car driven erratically because of a discontented family which couldn't go to the beaches on account of the deepening summer mist and finding any other idea too costly. I took a quieter road parallel to the coast, three or four miles inland. The trouble was, the mist here was even thicker, assembling in huge rolling masses over the harvested fields, extremely odd for a July morning, but far from unknown in this part of England.

Then the second dangerous and incongruous thing to happen in this July occurred; and counting Trevor's behaviour with his microlite and Greg's willingness to see me drowned, I was tempted to see it as the third attempt by someone at taking my life, or at least at putting me at high risk of injury.

I became aware of another vehicle behind me, rudely close to my tail. But it was only when the flashing started that I looked at it seriously, wondering whether it was something genuinely urgent the driver wanted to convey – or whether it was just another lout wanting me to drive faster and get out of his path. Admittedly the mist reduced visibility to about fifteen yards, but we were on a perfectly straight, reasonably wide stretch, I was not travelling fast, and the lout could easily have overtaken me. He was also driving a faster car than mine, a Volvo estate.

Now he was hooting as well as flashing. An emergency? A warning? Or sheer unmotivated hooliganism, motorised aggression for kicks? Perhaps there were flames coming out of my exhaust? Should I stop, to find out? Something told me not to.

He was out to do me harm, I knew that when he bumped me heavily in the rear. The horn changed from intermittent to incessant. The road narrowed again here. I accelerated, took a bend too quickly, almost went into a skid but avoided it. The Volvo almost overtook despite manifest lack of road space, drew back to let an oncoming motorcyclist pass, roared up to my tail again. Bump. I shot forward. Bill gained on me. Flashed, hooted. Bump. That time I was sent into a swerve, brought down my left hand on the wheel as hard as I could, mounted a verge and thudded back onto the carriageway again. Another straight stretch, clear of traffic as far as I could make out in the mist. I put my foot down very hard.

This time Bill was absolutely determined to overtake. Wasn't he? He wasn't. Alongside me, he was not speeding up but just keeping pace. Edging me over to the side. Something scraped, banged. When I slowed a bit, he slowed also. If I increased speed, so did he. He was forcing me into the side, into the verge, into now all at once a very frightening long brick wall. I had no space other than the width of my car. A hot, smoky, rubbery smell had started. I put both feet down, at probably sixty, where the wall ended, and he still hit me. And rebounded. My passenger wing mirror had gone, the wing on that side had taken a fierce blow from the wall, possibly the last it would ever take as the car might be an insurance write-off now.

I halted. And at last he overtook. And churned into the grass of a wide bank twenty yards further on, finishing at rightangles to the hedge. Other cars were passing by and not involving themselves in this problem, whatever it was.

Bill got out of his vehicle, gave only a rapid look at the damage, and came at a limping half-run in my direction. It didn't take extra-ordinary insight to see that he was uncontrollably furious. I thought it best to stay where I was. The pain of something that had smashed, in my ribs, on my left side, was making itself evident to me.

'Where are you meeting?' was what he said through the window I had opened because of the muggy heat and just forgotten to close as a precaution.

Naturally, in utter confusion, I said, 'Meeting?'

He gave a fast sigh of angry contempt; really, the man's calm, correct character seemed to have undergone transformation into a kind of psychopathic wildness.

'Meeting my wife,' was the answer.

I think my mouth dropped open, but not with complete amazement because I had to wonder whether just a little knowledge of various small episodes with Jane could have caused this homicidal frenzy.

'Congratulations on your third adolescence,' he said.

'I'm not with you, Bill,' I replied with real innocence. Only later did I realise that Jane must have told him about our affair all those years ago and references then to my *second* adolescence.

'Not *with* me?' Mockingly. 'You soon bloody will be with me. What about the lighthouse? What about Dibdin Street? What about those lunchtimes in the house?'

'Bill, I don't know what you're saying.'

'Don't know what I'm saying?'

I must have looked convincingly bewildered. I *was* bewildered. Slowly it came to me, though, that Bill was on the right track but with the wrong person. Jane must have confessed a mass of detail but held back on the name of the individual concerned. Bill had guessed it might be me. And who could the correct individual be, other than –?

I felt the pain in my ribs on the left again, and knew that my recent reading glasses had broken in the breast pocket of my shirt. Having forgotten to fasten my safety belt, I was relieved to know it was nothing worse.

'I've never been to the lighthouse,' I said.

'Oh no!' Not with this?' He produced from his pocket a mortice lock doorkey. 'You're saying you've never had one of these from Terry Fortescue? I've been and checked. This opens the museum door. And it's going in the sea. She's thrown things of mine in the sea.'

'I've never – *never* – set foot in the lighthouse. Who's Terry Fortescue?

Bill was about to say something more, but checked himself.

'But – you can't deny it. You know what I'm referring to.' A last challenge.

'I've not the least notion what you're referring to.'

He looked at me for several long seconds, then looked back at his car. Both nearside wings had taken a deal of damage. The passenger window had shattered. We had both been lucky to escape death by impact or fire.

I had to take the initiative, I could see that.

'Let's go and look at it.'

✳

I didn't have delayed shock. I had delayed exhaustion. That afternoon, on a high of relief at escaping a serious, even a fatal 'accident', I went straight into Consumerama, where everything was going cheap in a Grand Closing Down Sale and bought a pair of rough-and-ready reading glasses from the rack.

But my eyes were tired out within moments of starting to re-read

Rachel's letter. I should need to go back to Dr Koning all over again. Suddenly I was waking up fully-clothed on my bed in complete darkness, the phone ringing and ringing downstairs. I took in Rosie's photo on the wall and answered wondering whether she was calling me yet again.

'Hi, it's me. I had to be at work.' Jane. 'Where the hell have *you* been? I've tried eight – nine – times. Bill knows the lot now, don't worry... Mike, are you all right? We've had an evening concert, it's just finishing. I could leave in a minute and come round.'

'What about Bill?'

'Bill's in the hospital. Just for tonight, for observation. He blacked out when he got home. He *drove* home.'

'So did I, I think.'

'Ten minutes?'

When she ran in through the front door it was with all the old conspiratorial excitement; but she was plainly very upset and shaken.

'Rory and Zilla are out at a party and I've got to collect them, so I can't be long. I've got to tell you, after what he did this morning. He was coming to call on you because he thought we were going out together. He followed you from the house. But he does know who it really is now. *Was*'.

'I'm glad to know that. Who was it?'

'Oh Mike...*Trevor*.'

'Trevor?' The word came out as if I had never heard of Trevor, so Jane shrieked it at me again, grabbing both my upper arms. I knew I had been refusing the thought that someone as repugnant as Trevor Ridyard could possess a sexual faculty to tempt Jane with; it was something a civilised mind just could not imagine.

'So – he's been – Bill's been – aware for some time of something going on and thought it was *me*? You *let* him think that?'

'Well, not really. I mean – if he accused me of meeting you once or twice – I let him follow that trail because I knew he'd end up realising you were harmless and –'

'You used me to put him off the real scent? And delay his realising it was – Ridyard?' I was gratified, though, to think that

Bill had come to regard me in the end – this morning – as definitely not 'harmless'. 'I'm grateful for all this,' I added. 'It's nice to know he's got it clear.' Jane sunk her head against my chest in something that might have been remorse.

This affair had begun far back last year, before I moved into the town. Jane told me that of course Trevor was married himself (Ridyard had a *wife*?). Mrs Ridyard was abroad with the children (children too?) at Christmas visiting her mother in Spain, and glad to know Trevor had somewhere to go on Christmas Day.

Soon after the start the usual subterfuges went into operation. As Bill used the car for work most days, Jane and Trevor, both healthy and energetic people, rode miles on bicycles to their trysts while the weather was dry and warm. The thickets near the junction of Dibdin Street with the main road were one spot (where I had seen Bill's old blue bike parked with another last August). But in bad weather Jane might run back home from the hotel and Trevor join her from his office. Last autumn, though, he hit on the lighthouse as a less risky and more exciting rendezvous. He had a good friend in Terry Fortescue, the caretaker, who made over two spare keys on condition Trevor did not switch on any light in the building and locked the door securely on leaving. This explained the faintly flashing lights I had seen coming from the tiny windows around the top: Trevor and Jane were up there with pocket torches.

Oh it was all over now, Jane had no doubt of that. She had learnt a lot from it, and it would not restart. She and Trevor had had a tremendous row on the day I saw him in the microlite They had met among some distant dunes to which Jane had ridden by bike, and partly the trouble was *about* the machine, which she thought a danger to Trevor's life. They had parted in fury and gone off in different directions.

In defiance, Trevor had taken the microlite out of its rented shed and flown off in search of her. Probably because she told Trevor too, about our own affair at the Polytechnic, Ridyard had the impression that *I* represented a danger to their relationship: a case of ordinary, tedious (and murderous, I thought?) jealousy. When he couldn't

170

trace her from the skies he flew back over the beach, landed for a few minutes to check the dodgy engine, took off again, saw me, and brought the microlite down again on the beach to give me a good fright.

'So that's *two* men who could have killed me because you let them think that -'

'Trevor never *really* believed anything, Mike, please – you can't think that of me.'

'Oh no, why can't I?' I felt more sorry for Bill, though, and added, to make her feel truly bad about something, 'I can see what drove Bill to taking those photos and videos.'

'Oh, he didn't.'

'What do you mean, "He didn't"?'

'I made up a lot of that to distract *you* from me and Trevor. I couldn't bear to think of *you* knowing about us – I didn't want to lose you, Mike, I'm just so *fond* of you.'

'But we watched a video that Bill – '

'That wasn't Bill's work. It's one the girls were watching up in Zilla's bedroom at Christmas. Treazy brought it and left it behind. You remember Treazy?'

'You're not really telling me Bill never took loads of snaps and – you never showed me any, but you said he – '

'There weren't any. Or not *really*.'

That grain of uncertainty about the answer puzzled me.

'But Bill used to acquire photography magazines?'

'Oh yes, he did that.' Jane laughed. 'He certainly did that.'

Then she pressed herself into my arms; tired, I thought, wanting consolation and friendship at the end of a grotesque passage of her life, if I could believe the affair with Trevor was positively over. I embraced her warmly, thoroughly, for a few minutes. Then I said,

'What happens now?'

She drew apart.

'Oh Mike, you are so good, such a *good*, such an *understanding* man. I do need you so badly. You're the very oldest friend I still have.'

'But what *happens*?' I drew her close again; touched her, intimately.

'Nothing happens this minute,' she said. 'I've got to collect the kids.'

✳

All that anybody found out was that Geoff Stedman did have an air ticket for somewhere for that week-end after he had taken his revenge on Torridge and Underhill. For some place of temporary escape or refuge, if not necessarily a Greek island.

He was departing from a very modern airport which had unmanned 'transits' gliding you down from the check-in to the ultimate departure lounge with an automatic voice reacting to your inadequacies: 'Please hold tight!', 'Do not obstruct the action of the doors!' But Stedman did not reach the transits, or even the check-in desks. Having driven to the airport (his car was located later) he lugged his week-end suitcase towards its lights in the summer darkness but drunkenly could not figure out which way to proceed from the grass surrounds of the car park so as to enter the terminal. The place was almost brand-new, and badly signposted, and all state-of-the-art technology, highly confusing for him.

In a stupor of alcohol, and in baffled rage at the thought that he was expected to behave like a marionette on so many electronic strings, he blundered around the dark fringes of the airport complex and gained access to a set of indoor stone steps via a door through which he saw a group of similarly confused passengers emerging. It seemed they were arrivals who had been quite unable to find the official Way Out. One of them held the forbidden entry door open for Stedman, allowing him what was not intended, access from the outside through an Emergency Exit.

This remote stone staircase actually led straight down to the track on which the transits ran, conveying passengers to their departure lounges. At its foot, Stedman passed through a second door and saw a lighted sign, a little effortfully running man, white on a green background. This signified a way of escaping, if necessary, from the vicinity of a narrow, downward-tilting pavement alongside the track with its metal rails, one of them electrified.

Exactly at this point and at this moment, knowing he was badly lost but had time to spare, Geoff dropped his suitcase and felt in his jacket pocket for his cigarettes. To his relief he still had some. But he had left his matches in the car.

A fateful draught wafted along the floor of the transit track. In this gloomy tunnel Stedman could see that the breeze was keeping alight, down there on the stone pavement or ledge at his feet, a generous butt-end of a fag, cast away presumably by one of the individuals who had graciously held the Emergency Exit open for him to enter at the top. From this butt-end sparks were flying. But when Geoff stepped towards it he accidentally kicked it with his shoe and sent it rolling down onto the floor of the track itself.

It would have been lying there, glowing and sparking, about two or three feet below the level of the sidewalk, a tantalising prospect, Stedman's only immediate means of lighting a fag. Out of reach, but only by that few feet, if it came to it. About to burn itself down to its filter, though. And extinguish itself. Unless...

I do not know whether Geoff reached down from a lying or a crouching position and toppled or rolled over the edge of the pavement, or whether he carefully climbed down into what would be the path of any approaching transit, keeping well clear of the electrified rail. And bent down in that position to pick up the illuminated inch of cigarette from where it was lying underneath the rails.

Either way, the descending transit ('Only enter if you require Gates 1-12') had left the Departures concourse approximately fifteen seconds before, and Stedman was three seconds too slow and three seconds too late.

❋

'You want that *washed*?'

Ken Trench stopped, the grey drape suspended from his two hands like a cloak, as he faced me in the mirror with impolitely humorous amazement. I told him, 'Yes, I do.' And he replied, 'You're not worried it might loosen the roots of what's left?'

Of all the remarks, discreet or blunt, made about my condition by those I visited concerning my physical health or appearance – opthalmologist, dentist, barber – this one hurt my pride most. I had been quite determined to present myself to Rosie – or anyone else, for that matter – at my best this week-end, my hair washed and cut, my clothes clean and pressed, my house tidy and cheerful. Making an effort, I was rewarded with a comment like that... I couldn't manage even the beginnings of a sad smile.

'I'm not worried, no.'

Ken shook his head in wonderment and fastened the sheet under my chin. He should have been grateful that I had come. On a brilliantly sunny August Saturday morning he had no one in his shop except for one eleven year-old boy already in the chair.

Not that I didn't have to wait. The boy needed a long time to have his hair washed, and cut, and modelled, and fussed over, and shown to him in the wall mirror from every angle at which Ken's hand glass could be tilted. Perhaps an understandable irritation with this rigmarole accounted for the sarcasm of his question.

I had used the waiting time to good purpose, though, tearing open Rachel's thick manila envelope with a curiosity that surprised me, unfolding the typed sheets it contained, reading the ten or twelve poems she had sent. A yellow post-it note attached to them said simply,

> *Jill (Jardine) says I should definitely show these to other*
> *people. You are the first. See you very soon now!*
> *Love and kisses as always,*
> *Rachel.*
> *xxxxx*

Earlier, in referring to poor Geoff's teaching devices in the Polytechnic, I confessed to having no judgement in the matter of poetry, being a specialist in Politics; in which discipline it doesn't profit you much to attempt judgements, because you will invariably get them wrong. But I felt very prepared to judge Rachel's work as extremely promising.

We all, don't we? – well I do, certainly – know those moments when small sights, or little things happening to you, combine with mysteriously deep feelings you can't define, and you think there must be some way of *expressing* that. But if you try, you can't do it. Then you find that someone has done it already, much better than you could yourself. And said extra and better things about it. That person is a poet, or at any rate someone who loves, respects and uses language at a higher and truer level than politicians and TV commercials ever use it. That was how Stedman used to speak about it.

These poems of Rachel's somehow connected for me, too late, with Stedman's commitment, his loathing of compromise, of what he called 'compacts with mediocrity.' They were raw in expression, and she had forgotten to use any full stops (unless that was on purpose), but I could tell they had a little bit of the 'life' Geoff always said he required of 'art.' They were not only about nature and the environment, they were about herself and her problems, but not sloppy or embarrassing. If only I could have shown them to Stedman; he would have been the person for Rachel to discuss them with, not me.

'What's the future of a holiday town like this?' I asked Ken as he lifted my dripping nearly bald head from his wash basin and patted its hirsute fringes with a warm towel. I wanted an opinion from a local expert to help me think out where Rosie and I might live after the summer.

'Look at what's under your nose. That water.' He pointed down into the porcelain bowl with a free finger. 'It's going down the drain.'

'What makes you say that?'

'This parade for a start. It's not just me that won't be able to afford the new rents. The chemist can't. *Consumerama* can't.' I had

175

noticed how several of the smaller shops were closing, and boarding themselves up; in these early years of the 1990s the back streets were starting to look like a ghost town. But the passing of Consumerama still surprised me.

'What will happen to the Consumerama premises?' I asked him.

'You never heard of HyperCentresUK? They're coming. HyperCentreTruro. HyperCentreRochester.'

I had to shake my head as he smoothed down the hair on its sides with a very small comb.

'Bloody great air-conditioned atriums with escalators and fountains,' he went on. 'Multi-screen soft porn cinemas. Any fast food you like as long as it's burgers. Nothing useful. No grocers. No bakers. No barbers.'

'How soon will that happen?'

He laughed. 'Oh, it will take a while. There'll be a few more Black Wednesdays before you see one here. But they've acquired the land, so they can afford to wait.'

'What about the young people in the town?'

Ken grimaced this time.

'You saw that little lad I was doing before you? They're all like that. The parents don't have to chivvy them to get their hair cut, they come on their own and insist on the latest. The boys make more fucking fuss about their hair than grown women know how to.'

'What's "the latest"?'

'A "Darren Frognal".'

'Pop star?'

'You're *joking*! You never heard of Darren Frognal? The City sweeper?'

Next day, Sunday, I was patrolling up and down, from lounge to hall to front bedroom upstairs, anywhere I could get a view of the street. I felt proud of the way the house looked. It had taken time, but I wanted Rosie to get the best of first impressions.

I thought a lot about the shock of actually, physically seeing her. Thinner? Plumper? Different clothes? What if the handsome Christmas photograph had been an older depiction? Or just flattering?

She was late, naturally. Five turned slowly to five-thirty, six. The street outside seemed oddly still, as if it too waited for something.

Oh, but now, yes, Rosie had arrived. From the bedroom I saw a long car edging slowly along the gardens and stopping outside this house.

I didn't wish to be seen looking for her. I jumped back from the window and ran downstairs into the lounge, from where I could see her at the wheel. The vehicle was completely packed with belongings, crammed, stuffed.

Should I let her ring the bell or open the door before she did? I saw that unmistakeable shape through the translucent glass panels looming close – then backing away again. I opened the door. She, Rosie, herself, after this funny old year quite unchanged, was standing a few paces back gazing up at the façade of the building.

I had not practised any words to say in greeting. It would be best that they came spontaneously. I wondered whether Rosie had prepared a speech for this momentous reunion.

'It's going to cost us to get this painted,' she said. 'That's if we're going to stay.'

'Rosie!' was all I said.

'You're going to help me, aren't you!' Pointing at the suitcases and boxes and parcels which blocked the car windows. 'It was no fun loading this up, I can tell you.'

It was no fun unloading it. The contents looked as if they had been jammed, and stuck together for months (possible?). They needed to be prised and heaved apart. I took Rosie's instructions as to what should be carted in first, and where things should be put (after an inspection of the house and a lot of exclamations and some puzzlement about the fact that the top was in the care of an unnamed absent tenant – 'I thought you had the whole of it?'). There were not just clothes and personal chattels but items taken out of storage, I was sure: stools and pouffes and small favourite chairs, and curtains and quilts, and vases and wall decorations, and buckling boxes of crockery and miscellanea, and a bathroom cabinet to be fixed some time, and plastic clothesstands and rugs

177

and runners and radios. And a vast toy *dog*.

Having never lived with Rosie, only entertained her in my own sparse quarters in the city, I had not expected this much. In the space of two hours my house – our house – was transformed; so much so that I began to feel almost nostalgic about the way it had been. In the middle of the process I made a cup of tea we could drink in the kitchen while resting. I tried to refer to the importance of what we had done, looking at Rosie sitting with crossed air hostess legs on one of her own wooden stools. But she wouldn't let me start to express any of it.

'Oh, bags of time to talk!' she insisted. 'I'll have to teach you how to make tea first.'

When she called out to me from the bedroom to come and see how a quilt she had brought fitted the bed exactly and brightened up the 'mopey' colour-scheme of the room, I wondered whether it was a hint. ('Mopey' was a favourite word for something cheerless or depressing to her. 'That's a mopey attitude' she said to Geoff once, when he was taking a characteristically puritan view of something. I felt sorry for him.) I admired the quilt, as I was supposed to, and I looked Rosie sincerely in the eyes and made to embrace her. She merely returned the embrace briefly, and disengaged herself. 'Well, *I* like it,' she said, about the quilt.

She had bought and brought other things for me personally; including some new pyjamas. I put them on the top of the chest of drawers. While Rosie was busying herself to prepare a meal for both of us (her lateness had been due to food shopping) I happened to re-enter the bedroom and found the pyjamas placed alongside her own nightdress on a pillow; so that settled something. We agreed to skip coffee after the meal, which was the best I had ever eaten in this house.

I shall be very sparing indeed with the detail of what follows now. The moral I drew from the happenings of the next half-hour rang a distant bell and I remembered what my father once said, some time after my mother left him: that the only sex act which had ever given him any joy was pulling pigtails in primary school.

First Rosie and I undressed, on opposite sides of the room. Not with passion, but matter-of-factly, shyly, folding our clothes with embarrassed care, laying them down neatly on chairs and pouffes as if we were designing to sleep; Rosie yawning once, mouth wide open to the gold crowns as if the deliberateness of the actions reminded her of that purpose. There was no half helping her with, half tearing at, zips, straps, buttons, belts, or elasticated waist-bands, no cross-purposes as pants or panti-hose were manoeuvred over wide hips and pushed down over shivering, goose-pimpled thighs and over knees and ankles and flung into corners, no stuff like that. We did not then kiss shoulders or bite greedily at necks, or lick ears, or smooth hair down, or ruffle hair, or find inaccurate hands meeting in confusion as we fumbled for each other's genital areas. We just sat down together naked on the edge of the bed on the new quilt.

From which point we were not sure how to get into a comfortable supine position. So we stood up again, pulled the quilt off, folded it, removed everything else down to the under sheet and lay down on that from opposite sides.

Rosie accepted a kiss when we turned to face each other on the rough, rubbery pillows, but soon gurgled an 'Mmm!' of protest, pulled her head away, wiped her lips, and said 'Wet!' She tapped a finger on my chin, then ran it round my cheeks and asked, 'Did you shave this morning?'

'I did,' I told her. And kissed her again, hard, with closed lips, several times. She put a smoothing hand on my back below my shoulder and we turned fully onto our sides to face each other, my left thigh meeting the length of her right and rubbing against it in a clumsy caressing movement. My left hand now again found her crotch and fondled the clammy lips of skin. Her right hand took it away again. In doing that she accidentally brushed my fingers against the erection I then realised I had achieved without knowing, and we laughed; and I withdrew my fingers and left her hand grasping it. Her fingers felt surprised, but she continued to hold, even move it slightly, from side to side.

That was the second at which our movements on the bed

definitively became something approaching a love-making. Rosie's tentativeness vanished. She pushed her whole body towards and onto me, rough breasts rubbing against the shallow hair of my chest, asking me by pressures of hands and beseechments of legs to mount her and enter her. I pulled the pillows out from under her head and flung them onto the floor; but she grimaced, and retrieved one from the carpet to support her head and neck. She settled herself in a slightly organised position, squirming her hips to be certain she was comfortable. Then she clasped my erect penis, pressing downwards painfully, at the neck of its ungainly bulge and directed it towards the cavity she was lifting up for it. I remember thinking that our problem was that in the past we had never made love often enough to have worked out a proper ritual for these stages.

With her other hand she fingered and flipped at her vulva, and frowned as I pressed and pushed at wherever her flesh might give and receive me. But I was either, to my surprise, too large to find and enter her with comfort, or else Rosie was too dry and resistant.

'What's the matter?' I said.

'*Really*! Don't you know?'

Repeated guidings, pokings, or shiftings failed to provide any method of advancing this process. My erection stayed firm, but it was as if Rosie had no point of entry at all in the close mass of hair between those long air hostess thighs, now spread and splayed wildly across the sheet in dismay. And because this was happening the first time we made love after our decision, it was not a good thing. We were not yet relaxed enough in each other's company to call it off and try again another time.

'Damn and *damn*! I've got to try and find something to – something to put on myself. The trouble is, it's all still packed.'

She drew apart from me, sat up, grabbed her handbag from the floor, found nothing, angrily dropped it again.

'Haven't *you* got anything?' she demanded.

'What sort of thing?'

'*Anything*.'

'I don't know. In the bathroom?'

Rosie ran out. I could hear her in the bathroom picking up and throwing down tubes and plastic bottles, cursing, exhaling loud breaths of fury. I also heard at that moment footsteps treading up the outside iron staircase.

Next, she had gone down to the kitchen. She was opening and slamming the fridge door, the wall cabinets, the corner cupboard. I heard her, as I thought, assembling packets and canisters and jars on the kitchen table. I heard the words 'Thick-cut marmalade!' and '*Bovril!*' and the noise of glass bottles being slammed back onto a shelf. Then there were several seconds of silence in the house; until they were broken by sounds not below me but above.

Something like a bag was being dumped on Rachel's bedroom floor, followed by two heavy shoes, so that the three sounds were equal in volume, three fateful knocks.

At last Rosie was running up the stairs again. And appearing at the bedroom door with a frightening greenish stain on the mat of hair between her legs; plus a jar and a teaspoon in her hand.

This angry and handsome woman was now resuming her horizontal position on the bed beside me and spooning out more smooth, watery, mint-and-apple jelly onto her pubic hair, where she was massaging it into the folds of her genital skin.

'All I could find,' she complained. The scent of it was so strong in the bedroom it was virtually a taste. She put the jar and the spoon on the floor and pulled me back onto her. Her idea did help. But in the first seconds of triumphant entry and relief all I could think was that I had only ever smelt this before when I was myself spooning it onto something I was going to chew and swallow and digest. I felt the substance sticking to my own hairs as I moved inside her, and wondered whether my penis would eventually emerge green.

And yet, as tension and anticipation increased, none of these ludicrous considerations were as strong in my mind as a series or a composite of other thoughts, all unworthy and inappropriate. The first, during a passing second of doubt as to whether I would reach a climax, involved the voice of Jane making her implied promise last Saturday night: 'Nothing happens this minute.' And then, as Rosie's grip on me with her strong arms tightened with her own approach of orgasm, I had the notion she was both rescuing herself and saving me, and I was back with she-whom-I-took-to-be-Rachel, and we were embracing to save ourselves from the late morning sea, our bodies were grating wonderfully together on the sand in the shallows.

And so, 'Flamingo!' I cried out softly, my lips against the pillow under Rosie's head. It was a muffled cry, too muffled for Rosie to make out anything she could have taken for a name. A minute later:

'What was that you said? When you –'

'I *didn't* say anything. Did I?'

✳

Rosie wanted to shop together, for the week, next morning. I dislike shopping, and I did not wish to start up the rituals practised by other couples. She looked puzzled, even hurt when I said so, but allowed me to describe where the shops were that she needed and take myself off for a coffee somewhere. She wondered, though, if we could go down in my car, as she had had enough of loading up goods and driving yesterday. I told her it was 'out of commission' for the moment; not that the garage thought, subject to their examination, that 'the chances are, governor, you've seen the last of this one'.

With a little ill grace she agreed to drop me in the High Street and meet me at the top of the cliff steps near the lighthouse an hour later. We could have a pre-lunch stroll on the beach. I wanted to get some air into my head after last night's activity.

I didn't only want coffee, of course. I felt like an early drink with it. And a chat with a friend.

Sid Burgess greeted me with a welcoming wave across the Variety Bar, empty at 10.45 a.m. on a Monday.

'My turn this time, honestly.' He bought me a double, the first time anyone had treated me to a drink since I took up residence in this resort. He took one as well, which I thought told me something

182

about him. 'Everything go smoothly?' he asked. With perfect courtesy and discretion. At our age you were asking about the practicalities with such a question, not hinting at the sex.

'Yes, really,' I answered. His quick glance at me over the drinks hinted that he was thinking 'No better than that?' But he forbore to ask.

'In the end I knew my own mind,' I said. He nodded, several times. Went on nodding. Ended by saying, 'I may have got there faster than you.'

I did not understand him, must have shown it.

'I could say,' he continued, 'I looked in my mirror a few years back and saw myself for the first time. And knew I'd settle for this kind of job. Except it wasn't a mirror made of glass. It was made of faces. In my profession your audiences are your mirror. You saw us at the Horizon, you said? Not our worst ever show, but only one third as many bums on the seats as I've had years on the stage. And we went on and pretended you were thousands. Because you have to be professional until you die, or you die long before that. You reach a point where life is no more than one long hopeless performance before an ever-dwindling audience – and you carry on because life is all you've got and there's no place to go except on. If it had to be going on like *this* – ' he waved a hand at the bar – 'so be it.'

'What will your children do now you've set up here?'

'My children? Oh, my stage children, yes. They were just out of drama school, they usually are. They won't be coming here. My real children are middle-aged and in insurance.' He answered my next question even before I asked it. 'But Beryl *is* my real wife.'

'And Nobby?'

He shook his head and smiled.

'Poor old Nobby. Yes...' he sighed. As if that said it all.

When he resumed, he changed the subject.

'Look!' he exclaimed with a too-clear stage enunciation (but we were alone), 'You've told me quite a bit about yourself in these last few days. You've told me you're thinking of taking on this girl friend of yours you were double-crossing someone with for two or three years. And you're fifty-nine. Well my advice is, do it! When the lights come on at the end of another year, you'll be glad.' Was Sid quoting something he used to sing? Quoting, anyway.

Then he continued, 'If someone walked across this room and said, "You look like a decent bloke, here's a tenner," you'd think he was a joker, or a lunatic, or a con man. Or making some undesirable proposition. But − I tell you − I'd take his tenner, I really would. And thank him. And run. Are you with me?' He half-turned to where Beryl was calling him at the door, then turned back; and to me alone gave a wink intended to be seen at the back of the gallery, saying very quietly, 'And *keep* running."

I walked back very slowly along the top to where I was meeting Rosie. Rare conversation about life, and work, and purpose, and settling for what you were offered, made me think that Stedman would not have been as philosophical as my new friend, exemplar, and mentor, Sid Burgess.

As the months from Geoff's death lengthened, as various occasions brought him to mind, I had found I valued him even more. As, I accept, a wholly inert believer in certain political principles, an inadequate critic of the despicable politics of the last decade-and-a-half, a mere stay-at-home grumbler, I admired the way Stedman not only set his boundaries in a world daily becoming more cruel and crude and nonsensical but stood behind them defying the enemy. And enlisted me beside me, so that I could fumblingly connect my pusillanimous politics with his fierce cultural concerns.

For some years he had scored small victories against the advance of stupidity in the Polytechnic. Now I could not think of anyone left there to carry on the battle. Torridge's student dancers would graduate to whirl in corporate ballrooms, Underhill's middle-aged post-modernism would filter down via his media theory specialists into schools where children would be taught nothing more strenuous than the guiltless consumption of trash.

I realised I had, on my walks in this town, been regularly conducting the old 'fucking' conversations with myself. Hearing varied snatches of music blaring out from the CD and cassette corner of Consumerama, I would sometimes be able to recognise what I heard and react as Stedman would have reacted. 'Now what *is* that?' I might say. 'Ah yes. Fucking Rod Stewart! And that? O.K., yes – fucking Gershwin.'

Geoff, I only partially understood you, and confess to worse faults, but the misunderstanding and the wrongs that really killed you were perpetrated by others. I was your ally. You were what they call a secular saint. I hope your revenge gave them a little distress.

Now, though, it seemed that the acquiescent strain in my character affirmed by the realism of Sid had won out over Stedman's fury, by virtue, I suppose, of my respect for Burgess's dogged persistence with life. Later I would work all this out, no time now, there was Rosie striding across the green by Jane and Trevor's lighthouse, grabbing my hand and claiming me as we descended the steps to the esplanade, down to this popular end of the beach nearest to the town and the harbour. She had said a long walk wouldn't suit her today, she wasn't wearing the right shoes, but a short stroll would be fine.

We zigzagged between holiday families encamped on blankets behind windshields, and talked about the house. No, she didn't like it any more than I did. But whereas I favoured finding somewhere better we could afford to buy as a permanent home in the locality, she seemed set on moving out altogether in the autumn. A clash of preferences was becoming clear.

Suddenly she said, 'Mike, what *was* that note on the mat this morning?'

'I told you, it's the tenant who rents the upstairs flat.'

'Do you know her well?'

'She's a neighbour... I don't know her *that* well.'

'What is it you have to talk about? She said something about now she was back, looking forward to meeting and talking about what she'd sent you.'

Rachel's note had been as brief as Rosie quoted it, a suggestion that I go up some time soon and do exactly that. Luckily the word 'poems' was not used.

'She's been away… We have to go into some ideas she gave me about the repairs that need to be done and settled with the landlord. It shouldn't take very long.'

'I suppose it's a custom these days – but all those kisses at the bottom…'

'I think that's just her way.'

We had strolled on past the last of the family parties sunbathing, playing, and picnicking and were coming to those long stretches only explored by people who exercised dogs, flew microlites, jogged, or just fancied solitariness. Encouragingly, Rosie started to take an interest in the colours and shapes of seaweed, the life of rock pools. Then she stopped, with the midday sea coming in behind her and turned on me what I knew was a meaningful smile.

'Mike!' she said. 'We are going to get *married*, aren't we? That was the idea?'

'It was the idea.'

'You'll think about exactly when?'

'We'll both think about that.'

'And decide quite soon?'

'Yes… Good God!'

I had seen something lying half in, half out of, a rock pool at my feet. Odd detritus of rubbish and death washed up all along the beach: smashed sea-birds, plastic canisters bleached by salt waters, rotted pallets, light bulbs, onions, planks, shoes. Around the pools at this particular spot the tide had also left yellowing froth, a glass bottle, a carrier bag, and something flat and rectangular, something like a thick book with large open pages.

Not a printed book. A photograph album. It didn't look as if it had been in the sea very deeply or very long. It had a stiff cover, once secured with a brass button which the sea had released. The black pages inside were soaked and clung together, but the strong cellophane which sheathed many of them had protected the mounted snaps. If I was careful I could peel the pages apart without tearing – Rosie shuddered and stood back.

The colours were still fresh, and every photo was of a different woman or girl. On busy pavements, or crossing city streets, or on the grass of parks, or on beaches in sunshine; perhaps even this beach. Mostly they were wearing short skirts, or swimwear on the beach, and had their backs turned, moving away from the camera. I tore one covering sheet of cellophane and took a couple out. On the back of one was inscribed A-, on another C+?+.

'What are you looking at that for?' Rosie had turned and taken a few steps back towards the town, as if this was the limit of the walk for her if I was going to mope about with dreck dumped by the tide.

'Just curiosity.'

In the circumstances – the album was much too wet and dirty – I couldn't carry it back with me as lost property, even rip out a page or two and pocket them to drop round and ask Jane whether... Rosie would wonder. I left it on the top of a rock in the warm sun. It would depend how high the next tide was whether it would be carried off and left somewhere else.

✳

Darkness.

Only the cool pressure of the testing frame placed on the bridge of my nose.

'What can you see?'

'Nothing.'

'Are you looking hard enough? Pretending?'

'Absolutely, absolutely nothing.'

'You have the courage of your convictions, and you are – correct.'

Dr Koning switched on the ceiling light again. Pressing a button, he changed the big, black, diminishing letters on the lighted box on the far wall.

'Repeat after me, Mr Barron: B...E,W...A,R,E.'

I refused to do anything of the kind and spoke the letters as I saw them. And as far down as I could see them. Failing at the final row.

'The bottom line, Mr Barron?'

'I can't see it any better than usual.'

'Like most people. They prefer their illusions.'

Two could play at this.

'Not you, I'm sure, Dr Koning'

'Quite true. Not me, I think. I have spent a lot of my life looking at my very last set of letters.' But his face was serious as he mused over his tray of lenses. 'I learnt them a long time ago.'

A different lens went into the frame. I still couldn't read the final line, and told him so. He reached for still another lens.

'I learnt them when I was only a child. In Germany, in the war.'

'In *Germany*?'

In the *war*, in Germany? But in view of his apparent age, and his German origins, why hadn't I thought of this before?

He picked up the cheap Consumerama reading glasses with something between respect for any optical device and deep disdain for what you could buy over the counter.

'Well, in Germany partly. But some important things in another place.'

He picked up my smashed pair of his own spectacles, one piece in each of his hands, and looked down at them in the most curious and unexpected silence. For a long time. 'And for me, nothing is ever wholly past history, either,' he said, without smiling. With an inscrutable seriousness I had never seen before.

'Another place?' I prompted, uneasily.

He turned and looked at me as if I ought to have understood.

'Well let us say "an institution",' he replied

I was left dumb. Unless... Obscurely I felt Koning was being – What? – What conceivable word? – 'Unfair'? With what I could only take to be a broad hint about a prison, or a special hospital – or some place even worse? And whether this was true, or whether it was some infinitely deeper, darker, more unseemly humour he was subjecting me to, either way I felt that something or other had been reduced to its proportions, or put into a perspective of some kind or another. Or well, something like that...

'How exactly did it happen?' he went on.

'What –? Oh somebody... I had to brake very suddenly in my car and was thrown forward with these in my breast pocket.'

'Out of their case?'

'Out of their case.'

He was at once his usual self again. No less formal than usual, but more easily humorous.

'My spectacles were close to your heart, Mr Barron? This time I will give you stronger frames, your heart needs better protection if you *insist* on not taking sensible precautions...' He shook his head and smiled. 'And the lenses will be just a little stronger still. You need to see the close things even more clearly than you did last year.'

We went out to his waiting room, and he sat opening drawers behind the desk where a receptionist usually negotiated these matters. Offering various alternative frames he himself held up a hand mirror to help me decide which I liked. I chose something very ordinary and solid-looking.

'That? Have another look. Yes? Fine, then. A wise choice. You are going to look very handsome, Mr Barron – as long as you are reading. Quite rejuvenated! Which reminds me. I have already seen the very tall young unemployed lady you recommended to replace my retired receptionist the day you rang for your appointment. The one who was prepared to commute from the coast for a job in this city. It is hard to remember her beautiful long English name.'

'Flam – Victoria Tillinghurst?'

'She will start on Monday.'

At the door, to which he showed me himself, Dr Koning stopped and put out his hand. This had never happened before, but then I had truly become one of his veteran patients.

'We will try for you as long as we can, Mr Barron,' he said.

'I'm grateful. But only as long as that?'

'What more can one do? We cannot cross the limits of mortality. That is the rule of things. If they tried to make death itself illegal, it would just drive it underground. On the other hand, if what your Mr John Maynard Keynes had said in the 1930s was not "In the long run we are all dead", which is true, but "In the long run they were all *blind*", I would say he was speaking for today. Although I would take leave to say that one day we may prove it wrong.'

I had had an early afternoon appointment. The rush hour exodus from the city had hardly started as I made my way back in Rosie's car. It was a day of lustrous weather, just like the one last August when I left Dr Koning's and drove so happily to the sea. So I was (and now I'll use the word) 'home' in under an hour.

Rosie was making tea in the kitchen. She came to the point very quickly.

'I've been thinking. When we *do* get married...'

'Yes?'

'When it happens – if you won't object – I'd like to go on using my original name.'

'You mean – your maiden name?'

'Oh no!' She laughed. 'No, not *that* name. The present name. You won't take exception to it? I'd rather not let it just go.'

'You'd really want to go on being known as – ?'

'As Rosie Stedman,' she said. 'It really would be strange to be called anything else.'

By the same author

NOVELS
The Way You Tell Them
The Long Shadows

POETRY
The Railings
The Lions' Mouths
Sandgrains on a Tray
Warrior's Career
A Song of Good Life
A Night in the Gazebo
The Old Flea-Pit
Collected Poems 1952-88
The Observation Car
In the Cruel Arcade
The Cat Without E-mail

FOR CHILDREN
To Clear the River (as John Berrington)
Brownjohn's Beasts

WITH SANDY BROWNJOHN
Meet and Write 1, 2 and 3

AS EDITOR
First I Say this
New Poems 1970-71 (with Seamus Heaney and Jon Stallworthy)
New Poetry 3 (with Maureen Duffy)

CRITICISM
Philip Larkin

TRANSLATION
Torquato Tasso (from Goethe)
Horace (from Corneille)

For a full list of our publications please write to

Dewi Lewis Publishing
8 Broomfield Road
Heaton Moor
Stockport SK4 4ND

You can also visit our web site at

www.dewilewispublishing.com